THE MISSING VIOLIN

The Missing Violin

JEAN BOTHWELL

Illustrated by Artur F. Marókvia

New York

HARCOURT, BRACE AND COMPANY

© 1959 by Jean Bothwell

First edition

Library of Congress Catalog Card Number: 59-10171

Printed in the United States of America

For Julia Norton Clemes
in memory of good times
shared in the house without
a willow tree and at
Charity Abide

Contents

THE MISSING VIOLIN

Characters

The Tennant Family—

Dr. Philip Tennant, the father,
Professor of Ancient Religions

Eve Tennant, the mother, a former
concert violinist

The Jays, John and James Tennant, twelve
years old, who keep the *Book of the Jays*

Barbara Tennant, fourteen

Abigail Richmond Tennant, seven,
nicknamed Mugsy

Martha Hammond, who lives with the family

Dhayan Singh, an Indian schoolboy

Gerald Fitzgerald Kelly, a young American
schoolmaster

Captain Evan Meredith, Superintendent of
Police at Rajahpur

1: A FAMILY AFFAIR

The Tennant family was packing up. It was a new experience for the four Tennant children. Up to the present—mid-September—moving had been only something that other people did.

They had seen close friends and neighbors go about the business of crating furniture and wrapping china into shapeless lumps of newspaper to pack in barrels. They had seen the big vans arrive and had watched the men stow inside them the rugs rolled on poles, the mattresses in dust covers, the standing cases full of clothing on hangers. There were usually tears, but most often mixed in were smiles of anticipation when the owners got into their cars and followed the vans across the country to a new home.

But the Tennants weren't taking any furniture, not the heavy things, and they weren't driving anywhere. They were packing silver and linen, a set of dishes and some cooking utensils, the sheets and blankets they would need for a year of absence, and several boxes of books. Their clothing was necessary, too, even to the point of buying a few new things all round, but that was all. Chairs and beds and the piano were to be covered with dust sheets while they were away.

The children weren't yet sure that they liked the idea, any of it, even though there still remained some of the wonder they had felt at first on hearing their father's news. Dr. Tennant had explained it carefully, in many words, but what it really meant, reduced to the plain bald truth, was that a whole family was being uprooted and considerably inconvenienced for the sake of one person.

The person was a young man named Gerald Fitzgerald Kelly, who had been chosen as manager and headmaster of a boys' school in a town in India called Rajahpur—meaning the city of kings—and he had asked to be allowed to spend first a year in London for more study. So someone had to be found to fill in the year at Rajahpur, and the Seminary Board had given Professor Tennant special leave to be that pinch-hitter.

Dr. Tennant's own enthusiasm had been clear in his voice. It meant a chance for research in the subject he taught in the seminary, Ancient Religions. After he had finished explaining, he looked disappointed when no one said anything. How could any of them say a word, the children asked each other later, when the news had been like—well, a thunderbolt out of the sky was the best comparison, though no one of them had ever been hit by a real one.

Not even the fact that they were enjoying a special importance at school because they were going away could quite make up for it. Their distinction was great because they were to make a longer journey than any child at Chalmers School had yet made.

But journeying meant leaving a great deal that was known and dear to the four young Tennants in exchange for many other things unknown and bound to be strange and queer. Most of all it meant leaving the willow tree, behind the big clapboarded white house where the twelve-year-old twins, John and James, called The Jays by the family, had been born, and later Mugsy, now a pert seven.

Barbara, the eldest, couldn't remember living anywhere else, though San Francisco had been her birthplace the winter that her father was elected Professor of Ancient Religions at the seminary in this quiet New Jersey town not far from New York.

Because of that election, Philip and Eve Tennant had come

east and bought the white house and had settled down in it a little more thoroughly each succeeding year. It had had to fit the children's needs, Philip's teaching and Eve's music. The house had seemed large enough in the beginning, but the willow-tree retreat had helped the children later, when students overran the study and music room.

The lawn behind the white house sloped a little, down to the bank of a brook where the tree grew. The ends of its drooping branches trailed in the water on that side and on the other touched the lawn, making a green curtain between the children and the whole world. Inside, it was like a house with living green walls. No grass grew round the tree, and the ground was smooth, so that in dry weather it was almost like a cement floor. When it rained, the light scattering of drops between the leaves was fine for laying the dust. The retreat beneath the weeping willow had no faults at all, and in time it became a second home.

The grownups did not intrude there, never came except by invitation when Barbara gravely set out tea on a birthday.

No other child came, either, unless asked to on a Saturday or after school. This did not happen often. Bill Evans, a boy from the Jays' class, had followed them home one afternoon and stepped through the green curtain, casually, as if he had been asked. He never tried it again.

This was the children's own special place where they could talk or be silent, play games, work, or sit without doing anything at all, and there was no one to suggest some other occupation, less pleasant. When the green branches fell together upon their entrance, they were enclosed in a bright, pleasant world. The four Tennants did not come together every day. Home duties and afterschool demands—play practices, Barbara's cooking class, the Jays' Stamp Club, Mugsy's Brownies—prevented that.

Barbara, now fourteen, had begun the playhouse, with the help of Martha Hammond, a family friend who had come with

Philip and Eve from San Francisco and had stayed with them
ever since. If Martha had any other home, no one ever spoke
of it.

The playhouse was furnished with chairs of several varieties,
a table, and an old wooden cupboard, a cast-off from the kitchen.
It held an odd lot of things—discarded notebooks, grass-stained
tennis balls, a set of Chinese checkers with three marbles missing, a deflated football, three sizes of Christmas tops, several
pairs of roller skates, and a pile of worn comics.

On a warm Friday afternoon just past the middle of the
month the children were gathered under the tree after school.
They hadn't been allowed to skip the beginning of the fall
term. It would help, their father said, when they got to their
new schools in India.

"Schools, Father?"

"Yes, I understand there isn't anything quite like Chalmers School there. But with so many differences coming up, one more shouldn't matter, one way or the other, not even a little bit."

He hadn't convinced them. They looked at each other with long faces. Grownups said peculiar things at times. But the children were forgiving. Grownups were peculiar only because they didn't understand how things were, and sometimes no one could explain anything. This was one of the times.

Barbara sat in an old lawn chair, sorting a lapful of socks, matching pairs toe to toe and rolling them neatly if they didn't need mending.

"We'll have to put this stuff in the basement before we go," she said, gesturing around the spot with a waving sock.

The Jays, looking gloomy, had spread out some homework on the rickety table. It had lost a leg, but it did very well as long as it stayed propped against the willow's trunk.

"We do every fall, don't we?" said John, who usually answered before James had a chance. "Not this early, of course." He threw down his pencil. "I don't want to work. I can't keep my mind on this stuff."

James clasped his hands behind his head and tilted his chair back as far as it would go without falling over. He looked up through the leaves to the top of the tree, where bits of the blue sky could be seen, changing to white when a cloud came along. It was a sure sign of fall when you could see the sky above. The old willow was beginning to lose its leaves. He wondered if the sky in India would look the same.

But aloud he said, "I shan't mind changing schools or not going to New York on Saturdays, or being seasick—if I am— or anything, not so very much, that is, if only the new house has a willow tree like this. No other house would be quite right for us, somehow."

"Well, I don't want to go, period," said Barbara, "but a willow tree would help. Only two more weeks. We're practically off now."

"Do they have willow trees in India?" John asked.

"They do in Kashmir," said James. "Lots of 'em. I read about it. But probably we shan't be going there."

"Where did you read it?" John demanded. "Didn't it say anything about other places? Rajahpur, or . . . uh . . . well, Rajahpur?"

"No, it didn't," said James, and there was a thick silence for a moment under the willow tree.

Mugsy had a doll's trunk in front of her on the ground, in which she was packing a pile of small dresses and hats. The battered doll they belonged to lay on her knees. Mugsy was the only one who had shown any real interest so far in preparations for travel.

"My teacher is going to send Father a list," she announced. "Yours will probably do that, too. It's for him to take to our next school."

"Schools, Mugsy," John corrected her.

"List!" said James. "What of? Mother's got all the lists we need now. A list of what's in every trunk, on account of the Customs. A list of Father's books. A list of the Victrola records, only we'll say gramophone out there, Father says. And there's one of all our warm clothes. The things women worry about! Don't we each know what we've got?"

"Warm clothes!" Mugsy exclaimed. "My teacher said that India is a hot country."

"Not all the time, not in North India, where we're going, baby," said Barbara. "Three months at least of cold weather, chilly at Christmas, but flowers everywhere outdoors. Odd, huh?"

Mugsy shut the little trunk with a bang. "Then I have to go and get my child's heavy coat to put in here. If I need mine, she will need hers." She stood up, holding the doll by one arm.

"There is going to be how-I-read on my teacher's list. And it will say if I pay attention or if I don't and how I do in so-shul studies." She pushed her way out between the branches.

John whistled. "I might have known. A report card! H'm! If it's that kind of a list, maybe we'd better do a little work, what say, Jay?"

The front legs of James's chair came down with a thud, and he picked up his pencil.

But before any work could begin, Barbara said, "Sorry, Jays, but there's something we have to talk about, and we'd better do it now. We might not get such a good chance while there's still time."

They both looked up grinning, and John asked, "Time for what?" but Barbara was frowning and looking critically at a large hole in the sock spread on her hand.

But it wasn't the way they treated their socks that Barby was worried about. She said, "We can't call that child Mugsy any longer. How can we explain Father's nonsense to strangers?"

"We can explain it all right," said John, "but will they understand? We do, because we've heard it so often."

He held his pencil beside his right eye in imitation of a fashionable lady carrying a lorgnette. He made his voice high and thin. He said, "What a dear little face, Mr. Tennant, a perfect miniature of her mother!"

Then James cued in, in a deep voice. "That little mug?" he said, as their father had evidently said it seven years before. "That little mug? You can't mean it, Mrs. Putney. My wife is a beautiful woman."

Barbara couldn't help laughing, though she frowned again when John said, "Mugsy! It exactly fits her. It goes with her freckles and her specs and her sorrel top hair."

"What else can we call her, Barbs?" James demanded. "Not her christened name, I hope."

John imitated Mrs. Putney again. "Abigail Richmond Tennant. Fancy that, now." He went on in his natural voice. "Imagine introducing her, the little squirt, to a lot of missionaries or maybe some British people or . . . well, anybody. Before you could say 'Ab,' she'd be somewhere else. I could have named her better than Father did. Mercury! Now that'd be smooth, real smooth."

Barbara said shortly, "I wasn't joking. Gail is sort of aristocratic sounding. We'll call her that." She said it decisively, as if the matter was entirely settled.

"Have you spoken to Mother?" John asked her.

"No, I haven't," Barbara owned, "but when I do, she will see how impossible it is not to change. I'm sure she will like Gail as much as I do."

James said slowly, "You might let Mugsy decide. After all, a person's name is sort of—well, personal. You know what I mean."

Barbara rolled up the last pair of whole socks. "If we were staying here, I suppose I could bear it, but we're not, and this is something more than personal. It's a family affair."

2: "IT'S ONLY FOR A YEAR"

A little evening wind blew the white ruffled curtains at Barbara's window. They moved gently in and out, and her eyelids began to flutter up and down in the same rhythm. But she forced herself not to go to sleep. She was waiting for her mother to come, as Mrs. Tennant did every night to each of the children's rooms, if she was not going out.

There were murmuring sounds of talk along the hall, which meant that Barbara would be last tonight. That was fine, though she was so sleepy. She could take all the time she needed to bring up the subject of Mugsy's name. She had been firm with the boys, but she expected some argument with the parents, though they must surely see this thing her way. It was only sensible.

Barbara snuggled into the pillow like a contented kitten curled up for comfort. It would be a good beginning for the year away to accomplish that change of name. It should have been done earlier, should never have got started, really. It shouldn't make any difference to Mugsy and it would help her, Barby, to bear the whole upheaval.

Someone was playing a piano down the street, a lovely, peaceful melody that drifted in on the night wind and kept time with the curtain ruffles and Barbara's eyes. She felt sleep coming, just couldn't stay awake another second and her chance—to talk—was going—and—

The peaceful tune ended in loud, crashing chords, startling the girl awake again. There was shrill laughter, and voices could be heard calling good night. The Duncans must have been having another dinner party. They liked company.

With the sounds the smell of smoke sifted into the room, and Barbara sat up in bed abruptly, as if she had been jerked upright by an invisible hand. She blinked and sniffed. It smelled as if leaves were burning somewhere. M'mmm. The first bonfire of the new season. How good!

She lay back again, and the pleasant smoke smell evoked a picture of the coming fall—the wienie roasts soon to begin and the high-piled victory pyres after football games. But her pleasure faded in a moment and she punched her pillow angrily. She wouldn't be here for any of it.

But why shouldn't she be? She needn't go with the family. Why had she been so stupid? She was surely old enough now to look after herself if some arrangement could be made. It couldn't be too late for that, even yet. The tickets hadn't come, so that hers could probably be canceled, even if the money had been paid. People did change their minds at the last minute.

Barbara was wide-awake again, her mind busy with argument and plan, imagining what it would be like to stay here on her own, with someone older, of course. Maybe the Duncans would let her live with them. Then she could come sometimes and stand under the willow. Just remembering the good times that had gone on there would bring the family closer. They were the ones who would be homesick. Probably there weren't any pianos in India or bonfires. She would have all the best of it. She would be here at home. Ah-h-h! She stretched, enjoying the thought.

"Barbara, are you asleep?" her mother whispered at the door.

"Oh, no, Mother, come in. I've been thinking while I waited for you."

Mrs. Tennant laughed and closed the door. "Everyone in this house is thinking hard tonight. I'm sorry to be so late, but

I had to decide several things down the hall." She sighed. "I'm very sure, without calling up the India Consulate in New York at this hour, that ice skates will not be needed out there."

Barbara giggled. "The Jays, h'm?"

Mrs. Tennant sat down on the bed and reached to switch on Barbara's reading lamp. She looked at her firstborn searchingly. "No tears! I'm glad." She snapped off the light.

"Why would I be crying?" Barbara demanded.

"I'm sure you don't want to go to India."

Barbara sat up and switched the light on again. She was smiling. "How did you guess? I haven't said anything, not to you or Father, anyway. And I needn't go. I've got it all planned."

She searched her mother's face in her turn, trying to see if it would do any good to beg to stay. But there was only a queer look that she couldn't read, so she hurried into her plea.

"I needn't go, Mother, if you'd only see it my way." She was talking too fast, but the words came pouring out and she couldn't hold them back. "They'll take my ticket back, won't

they? I could stay with the Duncans. I'm sure they'd have me. They like people around. And then I wouldn't miss anything the kids do here in high school. And all the fun. Please, Mother. It's only for a year, anyway."

Mrs. Tennant had managed to smile by that time, and she sat shaking her head at every phrase of her daughter's argument. Finally she laid a warm, gentle hand on Barbara's mouth and made her lie back on the pillow. The tears she had been expecting from her daughter glittered in her own eyes for a moment before she brushed them away.

"No and no and no, dear. Hush now and listen to me. How could you think we'd separate the family, even if it is only for a year? We need our big girl. The more we talked, the less we liked any plan that would divide us, even at the very beginning. We thought once that we'd leave all of you here with Martha."

"Never," Barbara almost shrieked. "How could you?"

Mrs. Tennant said, "You see? The shoe on the other foot, maybe? I couldn't do that, so don't worry. It would be too hard on Martha. But your father comes first in this, darling, and you must see it that way. He will be able to meet Indian scholars in their own land and get their religious views firsthand. Even if he does have to supervise the boys' school, he will have time for his research, too. It's being planned that way for him. Think of the priceless opportunity."

There was only a sniff from the bed for answer.

"Barby dear, we discussed every possibility long before we told you about it. Father won't go without the family, and he should go. Every talk ended in all going or all staying."

"Bother that Mr. Kelly," Barbara exclaimed. "He probably knows enough already. Gerald Fitzgerald Kelly. It's too much name. He sounds biggity to me."

"No, only an American descendant of an old Irish family, proud of its name. You can't dislike him before you see him. That's unfair."

There was a small silence while Barbara pouted. This wasn't turning out at all as she had excitedly hoped. Her big plans were ruined, had fallen flat as a pancake. But perhaps she could win something out of this disaster. If she had to go, there was still the hope of changing Mugsy's name.

Mrs. Tennant drew her feet up on the bed and hugged her knees comfortably. "I wish we were on the ocean now," she said, "with all this packing and last-minute business behind us, though I don't anticipate a comfortable journey on the Atlantic. The tickets came today, and they've given us only two small cabins—for seven people."

"Seven! Of course, Martha. Can't she go and stay with her own people while we are away? It's bad enough that we have to go. But why must she? Aren't we ever going to be by ourselves?"

Mrs. Tennant said, "Martha is 'ourselves,' child. Don't try, ever, to eliminate Martha from any Tennant doing. I know she's bossy sometimes. But she kept me from making a great mistake once, when you were only a baby, and I will owe her that to my dying day. If it hadn't been for Martha, we wouldn't be here in this house now, wouldn't have had the twins or Mugsy, nor your precious willow tree. Nothing."

"What happened, Mother? Tell me. It sounds like a story."

"A dull one," said Mrs. Tennant, rising. "Go to sleep now, and tomorrow things will look different. I need you to help me with the packing, remember."

She was almost out of the door. Barbara said, "Wait, Mother, there's something else. We've decided that now would be a good time to change Mugsy's name. We talked it over under the willow tree this afternoon. Mugsy! Did you ever really listen to the way it sounds? Awful, just. How could you let it get started?"

"One of those family things, Barby dear. It just happened. And I was glad for her to have a nickname. Her own is a little long, and I didn't choose that, either. Your father named her. He has a forgiving nature." She hesitated, and Barbara waited for the explanation that didn't come. Mrs. Tennant asked, instead, "But why is it so important to change Mugsy's name now?"

"It's the best time, Mother," said Barbara patiently, as if their positions were reversed and she was explaining something to a stupid child. "We'll be getting practice in using the new name among strangers. That will make it easier, though, because then we shan't have to explain how she got her nickname. We thought Gail would be nice and easy, too, and . . ."

Barbara had never before seen the expression that showed plainly on her mother's face now, so shocking that she didn't finish her sentence. The mouth was tight, the eyes hard, the whole face stormy and angry, almost hateful.

"Never! Never that!" Mrs. Tennant exclaimed. "I won't have it. Does Mugsy know about this?"

"N-n-no, not yet, Mother."

"Well, it's her business, more than anyone's. She's a person, though only seven. But she shan't be Gail, even if she wants it. Never."

"Mother!"

"I mean it, though you do have a point. I hadn't thought of it like that. It does sound—oh, why did you bring it up? As if I hadn't enough to worry me, as it is. Oh—"

She whirled out of the door without saying good night and without closing it, and her footsteps on the stairs were angry taps.

Barbara's heart thumped heavily. What had she stirred up? Why had their mother allowed Mugsy to be christened that long name if she disliked it so? She had said, "Your father named her. He has a forgiving nature." What was there to forgive? And what kind of mistake had the lovely Eve Tennant wanted to make, long ago, that Martha had prevented?

Eve Tennant was a lovely mother, Barbara thought loyally. She was little and pretty but sensible too, most of the time, except that she hated to carry keys and a purse and was always getting locked out or locked in or walking because she hadn't any change. Now she had hinted at something strange twice this evening. What she had said must definitely be talked over under the willow tree, though without including Mugsy. She was far too young.

Barbara lay frowning and thinking. Fine people didn't make mistakes. Their mother couldn't play her violin the way she did, really wonderful playing everyone said, if she weren't fine inside. Then why would Martha have had to stop her from making a bad mistake? What did she do to stop her?

Martha. Martha Hammond. Stern-looking sometimes. Never good-looking, not in a stylish way, but in a good way, yes. But bossy! No argument there, but when one thought of it, it would be difficult to imagine the family without her. Nobody could make better pies. Nobody tried, because Martha was there to make them. She wasn't a relative and she wasn't a servant, but her presence gave Mrs. Tennant freedom to practice as many hours as she liked every day when her pupils' lessons were done.

The sound of *A* key, repeated on the piano, and the tuning of a violin, sounded loud in the quiet house, though the family was accustomed to it.

The Jays were still awake and they heard.

"Listen!" John spoke into the dark. "Is mother going to play now?"

It was stormy music that began presently, music that sobbed and wailed as if some human being were out alone, lost in the darkness and afraid. It wasn't pleasant music and one wished she would stop.

"She'll scare the Indians to death if she plays that way out there," said James. "She's all stirred up about something. D'you think we ought to go down?"

They slipped out of bed quietly and into their robes and reached the top of the stairs. Then they saw their father cross the lower hall from his study to the music room. After that the piano joined the violin, and the storm eased a little, became a gentle melody like a brook crossing smooth pebbles under summer skies.

The boys sat on the top step awhile and when the brook theme began, James said, "She won't need anybody now."

On the way back to bed they stopped at Martha's open door. She was turning out a dresser drawer, sorting the things for packing or leaving at home. Perhaps it was the way the light shone on her face, but the lines in it seemed deeper tonight, James thought, and her hair, which she refused to have waved seemed even straighter, or pulled into a tighter knot.

She nodded to them, so they went in and sat down on her bed, on either side of a pile of clothing.

"Can't sleep, eh? Want some cookies and milk?" she asked. Food was mostly Martha's remedy for anything wrong with a child, but they noticed she wasn't foraging in the icebox for something for their mother. She was ignoring the music completely.

"No, thank you, Martha," said John. "We were going down to Mother, but we didn't need to. Something must have happened."

"I know." Martha sniffed as if she was smelling something that had spoiled. "She never plays that way, unless. And there's some that could stop it, though I am naming not a name, mind."

She went on with her work, and when the Jays realized she didn't intend to say any more, even seemed to forget they were in the room, they went back to bed.

James stood a moment by the window that looked toward the willow tree, a faint blur in the starlight.

"Maybe this moving is a good thing for all of us. The house will be here to come back to. It isn't as if Father were selling it, or we were taking all our stuff with us the way some people do. Beds n'everything. But we aren't going to stay out there the rest of our lives. It's only for a year. What's a year?"

"Twelve months," said John.

"Aw, Jay, you know what I mean."

"Sure, sure," said John. "As much happens in a year as in twelve months. Sounds to me as if you weren't keen on this trip, 's all."

"Are you?"

John considered. "No, guess I'm not. The folks said we're going, so we are. But we don't need to tell them we don't like it. Right?"

"Right," said James. "It's only for a year. What's a year?"

3: THE BOOK OF THE JAYS

The Tennant family found the next morning that one didn't have to wait a year for things to happen. They could happen overnight. Mrs. Tennant surprised everyone, and her elder daughter most of all, when she turned to Mugsy and asked a question.

She spoke mildly, even somewhat hesitantly. "Suppose someone we meet on the boat or in England should ask you about your name? You will surely be asked about it in India. What will you say? It might be a good idea to change it now. What shall we call you?"

Only Barbara noticed Martha's startled expression and saw the look she and her mother exchanged.

Mugsy had no doubts and no suggestions. "It was special the way I got my name," she said firmly. "It's different and I like it and I'm keeping it. Let 'em ask. I'll tell 'em." She stood up on the rung of her chair and reached for the syrup pitcher and no one rebuked her. When she sat down and the syrup was safely spread on her pancakes, she looked at her mother roguishly and quoted, "My wife is a beautiful woman."

"Swell," said Barbara bitterly. "But just wait until your first date. Maybe you won't have any, not ever. Mother, can you imagine anybody taking out anybody named Mugsy?"

"They may," said Mrs. Tennant. All the taut, horrible expression was gone from her face this morning and she was a lovely mother again.

The Jays looked at the clock. "Whoops!" said John. "Be late.

'By Mother." They swarmed out of the door, with Mugsy at their heels.

Barbara was not in the same hurry. Maybe her father would help. Surely she was not the only one in the family with a little pride. Must she, only fourteen, be responsible by herself for the family dignity? Couldn't one of them see?

But Mr. Tennant's answer was only another disappointment. He refused to try to influence his youngest. "Mugsy's right, in a way," he said slowly. "Though I can see your side of it, too. But I wasn't thinking of dates and formals the day she was born. Little red mite that she was! Be patient, daughter. This will work out. I daresay Indian names will seem odd to us, and perhaps one odd name among seven won't seem strange to them."

As sailing time approached, each day brought new questions, and Barbara's anxiety about the dignity of the family was pushed into the background. She experienced spurts of interest in the preparations, particularly when her own wardrobe reached its turn on one of the lists. It meant a trip to New York City with her mother and the unaccustomed freedom of being out on a school day. It meant a new coat, a longed-for red one, three pairs of shoes, and a really super haircut, just the way she wanted it, after lunch at The Three Crowns, where the smorgasbord went round behind a mirror and where the Jays had never been.

But she was no nearer the explanation of the two stories hinted at a few nights before. Barbara was not so interested in new clothes that it hadn't occurred to her to try, in the closeness of their day's outing, to probe a little into the past. But her mother was skillful, and every lead was turned aside or interrupted with food or a clerk, or deliberately ignored.

"I'll find out someday," Barbara promised herself. "Something is bound to be told, especially if we watch. Now I'm glad, a little bit, that I'm not staying behind. It would be awful if the others found out in India and I'd get it secondhand. H'm. Not to be thought of. No, indeed."

It was the Jays, however, who did the most unusual shopping of all that was done in preparation for their year away. They were full of an idea at lunchtime, only a few days before sailing.

"Father, what does a diary look like?" John demanded the moment the last word of the blessing was spoken.

Mr. Tennant's mind was involved with fitting three males and four women and their hand luggage into two small cabins, so he said absently, "Oh, a sort of thick book with a stout cover. Who wants to know?"

"We do," said James, for once getting in the first word. "The teacher wants us to keep one. Of our trip. It'll be for the class."

"Nobody can read it," said Barbara. "You've never learned to write. What you do isn't even printing."

"Other people aren't supposed to read other people's diaries, anyway," said Mugsy. "I mean you don't. You shouldn't. It's not polite."

"But Miss Williams wants to read it. Besides we gotta do it now. Bill Evans said he bet we couldn't."

Their father seemed sunk in his problem again, though he was only watching Martha cut a large peach pie she had just brought in. "Is this the last peach pie we will have for a year, Martha? Or do they have peaches in India?"

"Apricots and apples, anyway," said John. "We found that in an old *National Geographic*. You'll be surprised what they have, Father."

"Thank you, son, indeed." He took out his wallet and held up a smooth, beautiful new dollar bill. "That ought to do it, at Woolworth's," he said, handing it to John, who sat nearer. "Diaries come under the head of education, if not journey expense. I'm still responsible for your education. I haven't quite figured out yet who is responsible for this journey."

"Gerald Fitzgerald Kelly," said Barbara scathingly. "That's who. Father, you sound as if you are sorry that you are going."

"Who in his right mind wouldn't regret getting involved in such goings-on?" Mr. Tennant demanded. But he laughed and winked at their mother. "Four females, three men, a mountain of big bags and little bags and stuff, and now an official diary, for cabins one and three on C deck forward, four days from now."

"That's easy," said Mrs. Tennant. "Get another cabin. And not just for the diary. You didn't count my violins. I won't have them called luggage. The diary and the Jays add up to one cabin. The girls and Martha and most of the luggage, to another, a biggish one, please, sir. And a nice little snug number for the violins, me, you, and maybe your shaving kit. See? No problem."

"They aren't exactly giving cabins away this trip, Mrs. T., but seven tickets do call for a little spreading out. There's been a mistake somewhere."

The diary the Jays bought answered their father's description. It was thick, and the stout cover was red, a loose-leaf item provided with two extra packs of sheets. They did not remark on the cost of those. They had pooled some pocket money for them.

"That's an awful lot of paper," said Mugsy.

"They'll need all of it," said Barbara. "If they write big, maybe Miss Williams can make it out. Ugh! How could she ever have thought of such a thing?"

They sailed from New York on October fifth at precisely three o'clock in the afternoon. The extra cabin had somehow been arranged. All the luggage was accounted for. And the Jays were particularly pleased with the size of the group that assembled to see them off.

When Bill Evans appeared with his mother, the family knew

why the boys had refused to have the diary packed. It grew very heavy toward the last, because of the extra packs of paper, so they took turns carrying it. But Bill Evans had seen it. That was worth the burden.

The Tennants' visitors went away reluctantly when the "all ashore" sounded, to appear again down on the dock, looking small and suddenly shrunken from the great height of the upper deck where the family stood in a row against the rail.

The gangplanks were drawn back into the pier shed, and the last ropes slithered down the ship's side to be secured by the waiting dock hands.

Water began to appear between the ship and the dock. They were moving. The ship was ready to go. And then the whistle's mighty blast made them all jump. It echoed from the Jersey hills, and the tugs answered, ready to push and hold back until the *Baltic* was out into the current and headed for the bay and the open sea and England.

Downstream the tugs fell back, and New York began to slide away, faster and faster. The Tennants were silent until they reached the towers massed at the tip of Manhattan, when Mugsy said, "Oh, I do think New York is the beautifulest city I ever saw."

But the Jays and Barbara had no words to express what they were seeing, a picture that blotted out the tallest building and the busy ferryboats and the beauty of the open bay. They were going; this was it, what all the preparations had led up to, this was what it meant to leave home and school and the willow tree. Its leaves were drooping this afternoon in the autumn silence behind the white house in Jersey. Would it miss them? Could trees feel such things?

At bedtime Mrs. Tennant walked in on an argument when she reached the Jays' cabin. Who was going to make the first

entry in the red book and what should he say? They were out in the real ocean now, weren't they? They should begin.

"How would you like Father to begin it for you?" Eve suggested.

Oh, that would be the very thing!

He came, grinning, when he was called, and pulled out his fat silver-banded fountain pen. With a boy looking on, on either side, he began to write at the top of the first clean white page.

> The S. S. Baltic
> At Sea
> October 5

This is the Book of the Jays, to be written about their fun and their adventures on a trip to India, where they will help their father and mother make a new home in a house that they hope will have a willow tree.

The Jays read it again after he had gone. "How did he know that?" said James. "About the willow tree?"

"Oh, Mugsy probably told him." John yawned. "She's been going into the study a lot with his slippers and stuff lately, and you know how she jabbers on. But she's not bad for a girl, huh, Jay? Not bad."

James slipped the chain in the bolt across the cabin door and switched off the light. He had drawn the lower berth for this part of the trip. He poked the mattress above him when he lay down. "Not bad, Jay," he agreed. But there was no answer. John was already asleep.

The *Baltic* was a fast ship and they were on the Atlantic only five days, arriving at Liverpool on the early morning of the eleventh. There were only two entries in the red book, one written by each boy.

From the Book of the Jays   At Sea, October 7

This is a fine ship. No Tennant has been sick. Mother played in a concert last night. She used her best violin. It is the one in the case with purple lining.

We have our own table in the dining room, but Mugsy was invited to have lunch with the Captain today. She told Barby the Captain liked her name. Barby was mad.

John Tennant

From the Book of the Jays   October 10

We are landing tomorrow. We are to stay about a month in England. Father is going to study at the British Museum. They thought they told us but they didn't. Now we can see the Tower of London and a dozen things people said we ought to see.

We won't know if we get a willow tree with our new house for weeks and weeks.

James Tennant

4: LIVERPOOL AND LONDON

There was fog in the Mersey River the morning of the eleventh, when the *Baltic* came into her berth at Liverpool. The Jays were disappointed—all their early rising wasted. They prowled the empty decks, shivering, and could not see across the river to make out what an English skyline looked like. The dock, what they could see of it, looked exactly like the one they had left in New York. It had a customs shed, and a gangplank had been wheeled to the edge where a wide doorway yawned beneath an arc light that had fog halos around it. No one seemed in any great hurry to swing it across to the *Baltic's* middle deck. Where was the crew? Where were the dock hands?

Then, from the heart of the fog a clock chimed with slow, ringing beats. They counted them. Six. It was that early. The Jays looked at each other and grinned. They had accomplished one thing. They were the first ones up as they meant to be. The crew was having early tea or coffee or something, no doubt, and a few of them were always awake. That was the way the ship ran. But no passengers were stirring yet. There was to be breakfast aboard and a boat train to London at ten. Four more hours. Maybe it wasn't fog. Maybe it was just dark because it was so early. And fog sometimes lifted. If this one did, they'd be the first to see what was going on.

They could hear the river water lapping against the boat, and nearby a truck motor roared for a moment and rumbled on its way. That was a land sound. Somebody was awake there.

James laid a hand over one ear and then the other. "I wondered why I felt so strange," he explained. "It's because the engines are still. I suppose our ears will get used to it?" He sounded doubtful that they would.

Before John could reassure him, they heard hurried steps along the cobbles outside the pier shed. A voice said, "I say, up there. Ahoy!"

The boys looked around, and there was still no sailor in sight. Whoever it was must be calling to them, visible in the bright lamplight forward.

James nudged John. "Be polite, can't you? Answer him!"

The voice said again, nearer, "I say, you two, this is the *Baltic*?"

They located the voice under the arc light. He was a young man, at least it wasn't an old voice, but they couldn't tell much else about him, partly because of the fog and partly because his face was muffled by his upturned coat collar and his eyes were hidden behind glasses with heavy shell rims. He was a redhead, the dark kind; they could tell that because he hadn't a hat. Oh, yes, he had one, but it was in his hand. He was wearing gloves, too.

John said, "Yes, this is the *Baltic*. We got in from New York this morning. Four, I believe."

"So! Will you then kindly go inside and tell Dr. Tennant I've come to breakfast."

He beamed at them and stood with his hands behind his back.

The boys consulted silently. Their father hadn't mentioned a possible guest for breakfast. But there was no doubt in their minds, not one, that the person peering up at them out of the mist was the young schoolmaster, Gerald Fitzgerald Kelly.

"He's supposed to be in school," John muttered.

"Barby will be plenty mad. What shall we do?" James asked.

"Be polite, of course," said John, "and then we can fade. We needn't see him. He has asked for Father; maybe they intend to have a talk alone. We don't have to tell him who we are."

He turned back to the railing and called down to the waiting visitor.

"What name shall I say, sir? Are you expected?"

He felt James's good dig in the ribs for the formality, but his face didn't change. Miss Williams said that was the way to do it, as James well knew.

"Fitz. No, oh no, I forgot, he doesn't know me." The visitor flapped a hand impatiently. "Say it's Kelly, Gerald Fitzgerald Kelly. That's all of it, entirely. Will you just tell Dr. Tennant that I'm here and that I will be with him when the means is provided? They won't take me up in a luggage sling, I think, so I'll have to wait for the stairs."

He turned to shout into the dark cavern of the dock shed behind him and was answered.

"They'll be coming along directly," he assured the boys, and added, grinning, "Oh, and if you don't know Dr. Tennant, the purser will find him for you. He's tall and thin they say and very distinguished-looking, though boys wouldn't know that, maybe—and he has a lot of children—"

"We know the man you mean," said John shortly, his politeness forgotten. Four wasn't a lot of children. The children sounded as if a family wasn't necessary—just along, like luggage.

James was annoyed, too. "You have to be a child before you're a grownup," he said. "He was."

They left Mr. Kelly to get the gangplank wheeled alongside, as they had no doubt he would.

"Fitz," said James thoughtfully, as they went along the passage to their parents' cabin. "It does shorten the name. But do you think we should call Father this early? It's barely six-thirty."

"We shan't have to," said John. "Look!"

A steward was ahead of them, knocking at the cabin door. He carried a tray. Early tea. They followed the man in and found their father up and shaving.

"Hi, boys. You're up early, aren't you? Have some tea." He waved his razor at the tray. "I had a wireless last night. The Kelly chap is coming aboard for breakfast, so I'll have to do my share of the packing now, before I have to entertain him. Wonder what he wants? Are your things ready?"

The Jays hadn't thought of anything but getting out on deck, when they wakened. Maybe packing would be a good way to escape eating breakfast with the schoolmaster. They'd get Barby to help them and that would keep her out of the meeting, too. Neat. They nodded, satisfied.

Aloud, John said, "No, Father, we haven't packed. I'll pour out your tea and then we'll go. He's here."

Dr. Tennant was rinsing his face, and he looked up, with water dripping from his chin, to ask with surprise, "Who's here? You don't mean Kelly, already? Where? How do you know?"

"Down on the dock, trying to get aboard. He said to tell you."

From her berth across the cabin Mrs. Tennant stirred and said sleepily, "Pipe down, all of you. It's the middle of the night. You'll wake everybody up and they won't thank you."

"Six-thirty and all's we-ull!" John intoned through his nose. "We're in at Liverpool, and there's a noisy fellow down on the pier who says he's come to breakfast. You'd better get up and do the honors, Mother."

"He calls himself Fitz. Very thoughtful, I'd say; it's so nice and short. He's done that much for us."

Mrs. Tennant groaned, but she sat up obediently and asked for a cup of tea. James handed it to her, and then they excused themselves, hoping their father would say nothing about being at breakfast on time. They could skip it or get a steward to serve them on deck. Barby would think of something, perhaps.

Outside there was now plenty of activity. Other passengers were beginning to stir, and stewards were hurrying about briskly with covered trays. Little heaps of luggage began to appear along the passages, and there were shrill whistles in the river and bumping sounds above deck.

"One more peek," said John, "before we go and pack. I suppose there's no use asking Martha to do it?"

"None at all," James mourned. "She'll be doing Mother's, you'll see."

It was lighter outdoors. The fog was slowly lifting, but it was no warmer.

There was a sign directing people to the lounge at eight for their disembarking papers. A part of the deck railing had been removed to receive the top of the gangplank that was slowly being maneuvered into place.

Fitz was waiting at the foot, talking to a customs man, but when he saw the Jays, he broke off and made a megaphone of his hands. He had to shout now to make himself heard above the other sounds all about.

"Did you find him?" he demanded.

John wagged his head, which was not according-to-Williams for polite reply. James added a long stare, and then they departed from the railing to look at the winches already in place above the holds, ready to bring out the heavy luggage. It would be fun to see the family's belongings appear. The whole ship had come to life in the half hour they had been below, mixed up with tea cups and politeness.

They forgot their own responsibilities and were astonished to hear the first call for breakfast sounding on the gong. It hadn't been any time at all since they had fooled Mr. Kelly. Or had they fooled him, really? At least they had been terrifically rude to him. What difference would it have made if they had let him know Dr. Tennant was their father and they would have no trouble carrying his message? And now it was too late to warn Barbara or to make any plan to avoid having breakfast with the family and the guest.

It was disappointing that Gerald Fitzgerald Kelly didn't show any chagrin when they appeared at table and were introduced. His eyes twinkled instead and he remarked, "I might have known you didn't come with box tops," and ignored them the rest of the meal.

Barbara tried to ignore him, but he wouldn't have it that way, and it was easier for him because he was seated directly opposite her at table and included her in all his talk of school and London and his plans for showing them about and for Rajahpur later, quite as if she was much older. The Jays would have been more uncomfortable if they hadn't known how useless it was for Fitz to try to be friendly with Barbara. He was the cause of all their troubles in her mind and he wouldn't be given a chance to defend himself if they knew their sister.

Fitz went cheerily along with them to London on the boat train and did not say good-by until he had seen them, with all luggage and two violins, settled into a small, quiet hotel across from the museum for their father's convenience.

"I shall see you again," the young man promised when he left, "a lot I hope, but today I've got to cut it fine, and now I must dash. This is a wonderful city and there's lots to take one out. I must see that you see as much as possible."

The Jays went with him to the elevator. "It's a lift in London," he said, and received their stammered apologies for their morning's behavior with a grin.

"You are a cool pair, I must say. I was annoyed for a bit, but then I remembered that I was your age once. Perhaps if you're very good the rest of the time, I can forgive you. An Irishman never holds a grudge long. It is too much bother."

"But you're an American, Mr. Kelly," John protested.

"So I am, so I am, but I can be both at times. And I am Fitz to my friends. You'll find it fits."

He grinned at them again—he seemed to do a lot of that—

and stepped into the lift cage. It creaked away slowly and John called down, "That was a very bad pun, Mr. Kelly."

"Your father liked it," the words came back, eerily, above the squeaking of the machinery. "You try Fitz. It fits."

It was Martha who asked the astonished hotel manager to have the enormous bed taken out of her room and a sofa put in in its place.

The manager was a grand person in a frock coat, and he wore glittering nose glasses fastened to a black ribbon. He looked at Martha condescendingly over the glasses and at the Jays who flanked her, one on either side, and began a protest—only began it, because Martha interrupted him briskly.

"This family needs its own sitting room. It's always a need where there're children and we've got four, sir."

The "sir" thawed him a little. He said mildly, "But you could use our lounge or the writing room."

"And can you imagine seven of us having family prayers in either place?" Martha asked him.

"London is full of churches," murmured the manager.

The Jays couldn't poke each other, but their eyes met knowingly behind Martha's back. There would be seven together infrequently for anything, they knew, from past experience. But Martha was a good arguer.

Both public rooms could be seen from the spot where they all stood near the door of the manager's office. The writing room, full of small desks and enclosed by a floor-to-ceiling glass partition, which ensured nothing but silence, no privacy at all, and the big lounge on the other side of the hall, a pleasant place with an open fire and thick carpet and furnished with many deep chairs. There were people in the chairs having tea at the moment.

Martha ignored the suggestion about churches. "Children make crumbs at teatime," she remarked.

The manager fiddled with the ribbon of his glasses. He cleared his throat. "H'm. Yes. Well—I suppose what you mean is a bed-sitting room."

"If that's what you call it, yes."

"It will make a difference in the price, of course. I've already made a concession to your number."

"You mean more or less?" Martha asked shortly.

"Less. We can't have crumbs in the lounge."

"I didn't think so," said Martha. Her tone was more gentle.

The manager looked at her, and a slight smile twitched his lips out of their firm line. He made a gesture with his hand as if to shoo them away and turned back to his office.

"It shall be done, madam," he said, over his shoulder, as he closed the door.

And it was, though why Martha should be inconvenienced for the comfort of the family, Dr. Tennant couldn't see.

"I shall be all right and it will be for the best. You'll see it in time."

They all saw, in that long month when they were becalmed between two homes.

There was a bright fire for them in the bed-sitting room on chilly mornings, though it was sixpence extra, and the mending basket was there, and the bright afghan Martha used for naps at home lay folded on the foot of the sofa bed. She had also brought several table games for boredom and rainy days. She smiled broadly when the Jays pounced on a new Chinese checkers board, set up and ready to go, when they dragged in one rainy October twilight. They had insisted at home that they had outgrown such a game.

The children scarcely saw their father in the daytime. He seemed to have established a study of his own in a cubicle at the museum. He did come back to the hotel for tea occasionally, but often the rest of the family or half of them were out, dutifully visiting London's many sights.

5: SEVEN TICKETS TO INDIA

Mrs. Tennant sat down in the writing room the second morning of their stay in London and outlined a daily program for the children, with the help of a map and a good guidebook found in the hotel's library.

"You won't be studying," she said, "but this isn't exactly a holiday either, so let's improve our minds, mine too. There is so much to see and we might miss some of the best if we aren't systematic."

"We are a sight ourselves," Barbara grumbled on the first expedition. They had gone to the Tower of London, the six of them. "Look at us, strung out along the sidewalk, gaping at signs and asking how to get to places. They'll all know we're tourists." She spoke the word as if it was a bad disease, something distasteful or embarrassing.

"But we are tourists, dear. What did you expect? Taxis? Or to sit moping in the hotel all day? You won't learn anything doing that."

"Well, please excuse me from learning in this fashion. Mother, it's awful. Look at us."

"I am looking—at a lovely family and at this beautiful city almost literally spread at our feet, an opportunity we shall never have again, with time to enjoy it. Oh, Barby dear, people aren't looking at us as much as you think. Come, here's a Lyons, let's go in and have some tea and buns. Maybe you'll feel better."

"Buns!" said Barbara scornfully, trailing in last. "You're get-

ting vastly English, Mother, all at once. We're Americans, remember."

"And you are being an extremely rude one, my dear," said
Eve, looking more patient than she felt.

Their search for places caused a little stir, even in a tearoom
so accustomed to tourists. Two tables with marble tops were
finally shoved together, and a pleasant waitress brought the tea
with toast instead of buns.

But the experience was not repeated after Barbara's outburst.
Sometimes, after that, Martha and the Jays went off together
and Eve took the girls. The next time they did a swift exchange
and each party was different.

There were sensible days of rest in between, when nobody
wanted to stir out, especially if the weather was wet.

"It is much better so," said Eve when they grumbled about
the weather, "or your minds will get too full, like a sponge dripping with water, and you won't remember anything."

The children were lounging in Martha's room one rainy
Saturday afternoon after lunch. Mugsy was practically breathing down Martha's neck, because she was standing close and
watching a dress for her doll growing fast on the knitting nee-
dles in Martha's quick hands.

The Jays were beginning a jigsaw puzzle and eying the glass
jar of mint bulls' eyes on the mantel.

Only Barbara seemed to have nothing to do, and she was
roaming the room restlessly, not yet settled to anything, when
Mrs. Tennant came in, carrying her raincoat and visored cap
that matched it. Her small umbrella swung on one finger by
its leather loop.

"Oh, Mother, where are you going?" Barbara demanded,
before her mother could say a word, though it was plain she was
about to speak. "Is it some place I can come too? There's nothing for me to do here."

Eve looked at her eldest doubtfully. "Only to the Tate Gallery, dear, on a sentimental journey of my own. It's a picture I want to see. This afternoon seemed a good chance for me to have a look at it, with everybody else nicely occupied. All except you, I see."

"Take me with you? Please, Mother."

The doubt changed to a twinkle in Eve's eyes. "We'll be taken for tourists, dear, for sure. No Londoner would bother going out this kind of an afternoon to look at something that can be seen just as well on any good day of the year. Besides, everyone who lives here must already have seen it."

"But there would be only two of us. Please, Mother."

"All right, run get your things. But don't expect to have tea out. Father promised me faithfully he'd join us here today."

At the gallery, Mrs. Tennant bought a catalog and sat down on the nearest bench to find the location of the one picture she had come to see, and then she went straight to it, without stopping to look at other things equally famous along the way.

"Ah, here it is!"

There was great satisfaction in Eve's voice and something else, some other feeling, deeper than pleasure at finding it so easily.

At first sight Barbara wondered why on earth her mother had wanted to come out on a rainy afternoon to look at just one picture when it was as small and unassuming as this one. It was listed in the catalog as Reynolds' "Age of Innocence" and showed a little girl wearing a yellow frock and sitting under a tree. The child was beautiful, but that was all.

Barbara waited quietly, not wanting to risk being told that she needn't have come. She began to feel uneasy and awkward, wishing she hadn't insisted, when the thought grew that perhaps her mother might have preferred coming here alone. As far as Barbara could tell, this was the first time her mother had expressed a wish to see anything, particularly. She had smilingly fallen in with all the children's wishes, even to separating

them into groups to please her, Barbara. She squirmed and her face flamed. Why had there seemed to be too many people on a London sidewalk when the number was just right under the willow tree in New Jersey? Why?

There were only a few people in the gallery, and the afternoon dragged on dully for Barbara.

After a long while Eve said, "It's sweet, isn't it, dear?" She went on, almost dreamily, as if she was far away. "There was a print of it on the wall of a room I once had when I was growing up. The print showed the fine cracks in the paint—see them? I loved that little girl, perhaps it was because I had no playmates just then. You can feel that she is going to a party or something special. I used to look at her before the light was turned off at night and make up stories about what she did after she finished sitting for the painter."

"You never told us about that," said Barbara reproachfully. "Where was that room, Mother? Was it before your mother and father went away—I mean, uh, you know, they died, didn't they? Or was it after? Do you know that your own children don't know any 'When-I-was-a-little-girl' stories about you the way lots of mothers tell them."

Mrs. Tennant turned away from the painting. "Probably because I didn't have an ordinary childhood," she said. Her mouth began to take on the hard line that Barby remembered from the night at home when they had talked about Mugsy's name. "Perhaps it was because there was so much to tell that I didn't want to begin."

"But you could start any time, Mother. We'd always listen."

"Would you?" Then she looked at her watch. "Come along, child; let's see something else in the time we have. They didn't build this big place just to keep my 'little girl' in." She tried to toss away their solemn moment, but there was a small quaver in her voice that Barbara did not miss.

They were not able to sit together on the bus on the return to the hotel, and Barbara had time to reflect again on the gaps in the family history. Her curiosity was only piqued the more, and she knew that she must somehow make an opportunity to tell the Jays—Mugsy wouldn't understand—what had been said this afternoon. There hadn't been an opportunity to have a willow tree talk since they had left home. They did need a place of their own.

At the museum stop in Bloomsbury the rain was coming in such torrents that they ran the half block to the hotel, with their umbrellas covering their faces against the wind, so that they almost collided with another refugee from the storm.

"Oh, I say," said a voice they knew, "you might look where you're going."

"Fitz!" said Eve. "What a start you gave me! Come along in and have some tea with us."

"That was my whole intention," he said, grinning at them both, but Barbara only looked severe and very grown-up in her raincoat and cap, and as if someone had suddenly thrust something disagreeable at her.

Martha had laid the tea table with a cloth from home. It was astonishing how many tricks there were in her bag to make that austere hotel room seem like the coziest home place in the world.

John lifted a plate and thrust it forward for his mother to see. "How could this hotel have plates like we have?" he demanded.

"Easiest thing in the world," said Eve, smiling. Barby noticed that the tight line was gone from her mouth. "Because we have English china. And these don't belong to the hotel. Martha went shopping for me the other day after I saw some in a window. I decided that we'd need more cups and plates if we had people in for tea in India. They say one does, a lot."

"And we might break a few," said James thoughtfully.

"Say it not, my son, not aloud and don't even think it. Not at the price these were."

"If you do have any breakages, I'll bring out some more," said Fitz cheerfully, starting to hand out the cups that Martha began filling from a big pot.

Mr. Tennant came in, dripping, and the conversation immediately stopped being domestic. Fitz could talk on an enormous number of topics it seemed, for a young man of five and twenty.

"He's just a show-off," Barbara maintained, whenever anyone was inclined to praise the young man.

When tea was over that day and there was a pleasant lull in the talk, Fitz said, without preamble, "I have four tickets for

the London Symphony a week from tonight. I can't invite all
the family with only four tickets to be spread among eight people . . ."

"D'you hear what he's saying," Barbara whispered angrily
to John. "Him, a part of the family!"

John glared at her for interrupting, and Fitz himself glanced
in her direction, though he couldn't possibly have heard what
Barby said, John assured himself uneasily.

"So," Fitz went on, "let's have a draw and see who goes."

He took seven slips of paper from one pocket and the four
precious tickets from another, and made some kind of hiero-
glyphics on each of the seven slips, after consulting the printing
on the tickets. Then he held them up, and each member of the
family gravely drew a slip after some deliberation.

Fitz studied the slips again, compared them with the tickets,
and announced the winners: Mrs. Tennant, James, and Barbara.

Mugsy said, "I wanted to go, I did, and sit by Fitz."

The family laughed, but Mrs. Tennant gathered the child
into her arms. "A concert is too late at night for you," she said
comfortingly. "Remember, at home you never went out at
night."

"But this is London," Mugsy protested.

"So it is," said Fitz. "And no where in the world do they have
better waxworks. So I've heard. That goes well in the afternoon. You wait; your turn will come."

Fitz had no explanation for managing to get leave as often
as he did from his classes during that month of the Tennants'
visit to London. He made good his promise of the waxworks for
Mugsy, but he also arranged an excursion for the Jays to the
Covent Garden markets at four o'clock in the morning, to
watch the enormous supplies of fresh food for London being
brought in and sold by the case and in van lots. Then they had

tea and buns standing up at a counter surrounded by red-faced van drivers and stall owners, listening to the market jargon and each clutching a Malta orange bestowed by a smiling stall owner when she found they were Americans.

They also carefully carried, each taking turns, a small bunch of violets selected at a flower stall after much thought. That was for Eve to wear to the symphony if they'd stay fresh that long.

Fitz said, "Indeed they will. It's only until tomorrow night."

Out of all their London experiences and the short trips they made into Surrey and Oxford and Warwick, the symphony was for James the highest peak, and his only regret was for the absence of the other Jay. Barby had tried to give her ticket to John, but Fitz heard of it and smilingly refused.

"Ah, now, we couldn't go against the Fates," he said. "It was your lot to have the ticket."

James confided the evening to the diary. John could have that much of it.

From the Book of the Jays   London
                                                            November 4

Three of us went to the symphony last night with Mr. Kelly. He got the tickets. Sir Thomas Beecham was conducting and we had wonderful seats. It was special because the Royal Family came. Mr. Kelly didn't know about that when he chose the night. Nobody can go home until they leave, and even if they weren't there, nobody can go home until they play "God Save the King."

I didn't want to go home when it was over, it was so beautiful. They played the "Emperor Concerto" and I don't remember the name of the pianist. I lost my program on the way home. It doesn't matter. I'll never forget the music. You feel lifted high up and then you feel as if you had come down to a little stream rippling along over stones, and then the cymbals and the drums go crash and you soar up again. It was wonderful. Sir Thomas took many bows and the noise the audience made was as thunderous as the drums.

It was tonight that we found out Mr. Fitz is a musician, too. He plays a clarionet. He said he wished we were going to be in India after he gets there and we'd have ourselves a little orchestra. But I said none of us cared to learn music, and mother heard and said maybe that could be changed. I don't know how. Real know-the-way-to-do-it has to be born in you, I think.

James Tennant

And then, surprisingly, they were in the last week of their stay, with reservations out of Liverpool on the S.S. *Castalia* of the Anchor Line, bound for Bombay.

Fitz came to tea a last time, and after that Martha began packing extras, and the new plates and cups and the afghan and the games were put away, not to be seen again until they reached their new home in India.

Mugsy had enjoyed the waxworks, but she was still grieving because she hadn't heard the symphony, especially upon hearing that the Royal Family had been there. "I wanted to see the King and Queen," she mourned.

"But I'd still like to know how Barby got to go, when everybody knows—"

"Mugsy," said Martha commandingly, "remember your manners."

"Sometimes I wish I didn't have any," said Mugsy, pulling her spectacles down on her nose. She looked so much like a cross old woman that Fitz shouted with laughter.

"I'll tell you how it was, little lady," he said, drawing her inside the crook of his arm so that she could lean against his knee while he talked.

"It was like this," he said seriously. "There were only four tickets, so there could be only one Jay."

"Yes."

"And the Lady Who Makes Music, she couldn't be left out."

"No."

"And there was me."

"I," said Martha, correcting him mechanically, as if he were one of the children.

He winked at the others as he said, "Well, Fitz, then, Martha-me-darlin'. 'Tis one and the same, or Gerald Fitzgerald Kelly, if you like, ma'am."

He stood up and made a bow to her, and they all laughed and no one noticed until a long time afterward, when it was too late to finish, that Fitz had neatly sidestepped explaining how Barby got the fourth ticket to the symphony.

The Jays were sure, the afternoon that the lots were drawn, that there had been something mighty queer in the way the slips of paper had been manipulated. The drawing hadn't had anything to do with the way the tickets were given out. But because Fitz was the host, they couldn't say anything. They pondered it later on the boat and got no satisfactory answer.

"Barby doesn't even like him, and he couldn't help knowing it, without Mugsy saying so, which was what Martha stopped her from doing," said John, shaking his head.

James said, "After all he is a grownup, though the young sort, and grownups do odd things, of course."

There were lowering skies on the day they sailed again out of Liverpool. This time they watched other passengers' farewells. There was no one they knew to wave to when the ship weighed anchor and went down the Mersey River to the open sea. At the last minute Fitz Kelly had not been able to get away to come with them to the boat. It gave the Jays a lonely feeling, which they did not mention to anyone. They had found a new friend, only to lose him again after so short a time. Barby was crazy not to like him.

Cabin arrangements were as before. They were the only Americans aboard, but it did not seem odd now to have "elevenses" and tea in addition to the familiar American routine of breakfast, luncheon, and dinner.

The Jays were usually on hand when the deck steward appeared in the late morning with his little wheeled tray to dispense cups of steaming broth. And they liked the crisp, sweet little cakes that he called biscuits, served with strong black tea at four o'clock. But they shook their heads when he offered them tea.

The steward shook his. "Now, now, you Americans. You'll learn. It's a fine bracer for this damp weather. And when we get into the heat, it'll cool you off. Nothing like it. No sirree!"

After Port Said they learned what he meant by heat. People came out of their blanket cocoons in deck chairs. Everybody was more friendly. Mrs. Tennant and Martha changed the packing all round again, and their thinner clothing appeared. The Jays wore cotton trousers now and sleeveless cotton pullovers for daytime. For dinner there were dark blue jackets with white flannels and thin white lawn shirts and narrow ties. They protested the ties, but it did no good.

The sailors rigged a huge canvas pool in the well deck, which they filled with a hose, and all the children aboard splashed there every afternoon.

Mugsy made friends with the whole crew, from cabin steward up. One morning John heard Barbara say, "Mother, I'm so ashamed. Everybody on this ship knows how that child got her name. Has she no pride at all? What will these people think of us? I tried to prevent it, but you wouldn't listen."

Mrs. Tennant laughed. "You mean Mugsy wouldn't. You are the only one who minds very much. Why don't you play a game with the Jays? You'll have a better time if you mix a little, yourself. Mugsy has the right idea. People aren't liked or disliked for the sake of their names, my dear child."

Barbara only scowled and refused John's invitation to do a round of shuffleboard.

John watched her stalk off, looking straight ahead, and thought to himself hopefully that Barby would feel better when they reached India, where surely the children could be by themselves again and talk things over in the old way. If only there would be a willow tree in Rajahpur!

It was a scorching hot morning, the third day of December, when the *Castalia* arrived in Bombay. There was no fog here. Against the unclouded clear blue sky black crows wheeled and dipped, cawing hoarsely. A great roar of sound, the voices of people, muffled a little by the customs sheds, came from the streets beyond.

From the ship's railing everything looked strange. Even the buildings were different from any the Jays had known before. They were made of deep yellow plaster, with white trim. Someone was pointing out familiar sights. That was the Taj Mahal Hotel, he said. And when the Jays took a second look, they realized that the trees were palms, only seen before in a botanical garden at home.

The coolies working far below them on the dock were almost naked. Their brown skins glistened with sweat in the bright morning light.

In the lounge behind the tables from which the green felt covers had been removed, white-uniformed officials sat. They conducted medical examinations, stamped passports, issued landing tickets, and patiently answered a thousand questions.

The family got in line early, but Mr. Tennant said there was no use hurrying ashore. They'd wait more comfortably on the boat while the heavy luggage was being taken off. There were piles of hand things everywhere outside the cabins and more appearing on the decks, ready to be picked up and carried ashore by patient coolies.

In the waiting time the Jays took their red book to the upper deck, away from the crowd and where they could look down on the unloading and note the new things they saw. They had been faithful to the writing, even when it had got so hot that the ink smudged and their moist hands left blots on the white pages.

They sat down together on a deserted deck chair. James flipped a few pages back and began to read aloud, recalling the fun they'd had in England.

London was there, complete as they had seen it many times through the eyes of Fitz Kelly, whose name appeared often. They had been lost in the fog with him once, and Barby had been furious because she had had to take his arm in the effort not to be separated.

"Fitz didn't seem to notice that," said John.

"It's because he really likes her," said James, looking up from the page. "You'd think he'd find someone his own age. Did he ever say anything about any girls he's met in England?"

John shook his head. "Barby's crazy. He's wonderful. It wasn't his fault we were the ones to do a year so he could get another degree. He does seem smart enough now, but he must have a good reason to want to study more."

"Probably," said James and went on reading. They had included the changing of the guard at Whitehall, the lions on Nelson's monument, the tall policemen, the thick eiderdown quilts on the beds in their hotel, and baths for sixpence.

And beyond London there had been the grandeur of the peacocks on the green lawns at Warwick Castle, and the coats of arms in colored glass let into the windows there. The guide was a heraldry enthusiast, and he had spent a lot of time trying to explain what each symbol meant.

The ruins at Kenilworth, seen in a late afternoon with dusk coming on, had been sad, and they were glad to climb back into the waiting car.

Next to New York, James thought, London was the best city

in the world. He wondered if he would always dislike leaving any place where he was. London would be a fine one to stay in a long time. And now he didn't want to get off this ship.

He read down to the two latest entries.

From the Book of the Jays   November 22

We are in the Indian Ocean. That comes after the Red Sea. It's very hot. Everybody takes naps after lunch now. Mother plays nearly every night. They like it. She uses the violin in the red-lined case mostly, because of the sea air being bad for the best one.

The Suez Canal is not a straight line. I thought it was.

Barby talked to us one night at the hotel in London when Father and Mother were out and Mugsy was asleep. It seems queer that we'd be almost twelve years old before finding out that there's a sure-fire family mystery. It's all mixed up with when Mother was a girl. Barby found out some when she objected to Martha's coming with us and Mother said we had a debt to Martha and that she would always be with us if she wanted to. Barby says the debt isn't money.

                                        John Tennant

The last entry was James's own, written late the night before, but he read it over, liking it.

From the Book of the Jays   December 2nd

We're almost there. I like sailing. I almost would rather stay on. But there's a lot to see in India. People are packing now. They go around giving each other a piece of paper with their address on it.

A sailor told Jay and me to come "right away forrad" after dinner and we'd see something. We did. It was Bombay. We had the first look. Way down low against the sky, lights that were not stars. You wouldn't notice unless a sailor showed you. They were signaling a message to the port. The machine made a pumping sound, spelling out the words. We'll be in before morning, we're that near. But we can't go up to Ballard Pier until daylight. Father said he didn't know when we'd be allowed to go ashore. I wish Bill Evans could see us now.

James Tennant

"I say, Jay," he said at the end, "we're putting down more in this than the trip. We won't want Miss Williams reading the part about the family to the class."

John said, "I suppose you mean the part about what Barby and Fitz and Mugsy said? You're right, but it belongs—what each member of the family does and the things we are all interested in. Only thing we can do now is to tell Miss Williams to leave those bits out. We can't."

6: ON THE BOMBAY MAIL

George Henderson, manager of the mission business office of the Port of Bombay, came aboard with a handful of letters for Dr. Tennant and a supply of Indian money. He also had brought their tickets for the Bombay Mail, going north at nine that evening.

"It will take you two nights to get to Rajahpur," he said. "You'll need a few things for the trip, the way we travel out here. Everyone goes shopping the first thing when arriving in Bombay."

He shook hands with them all solemnly, down to Mugsy, then pulled out a large kerchief and wiped his hot face. Except for its redness he didn't look uncomfortable. He was dressed in crisp white coat, shirt, and trousers. Even his shoes were white. He looked at the heap of luggage beside them on the deck and sighed.

"Seven of you. Well, we've had larger families through here in my day."

He went closer and examined the things, piece by piece, and smiled for the first time.

"Violins! Who plays? Ah, I did hear about that somewhere. It's Mrs. Tennant, eh? Eve Carmichael. Used to be a concert artist. Right?"

The Jays, immediately alert, saw their mother shake her head violently at Mr. Henderson, before she said modestly, "Not a very good one, I'm afraid. This family is—I mean it takes my time—I'm afraid I don't—"

Mr. Henderson said heartily, "Oh sure, sure, got to feed 'em, got to dress 'em, sew, cook, and what not. Having a family washes up a career. You aren't the first one."

He turned to Dr. Tennant. "I've got a man to attend to this customs business for you. There probably won't be too much duty unless you have something to sell. Mostly personal effects and household things, I take it."

"That's what we were told to bring," said Dr. Tennant, and his wife laughed. "I'm beginning to think we shall need all we have and more, too. No, sir, nothing to sell, definitely."

"Good," said Mr. Henderson. "We'll go to my house for lunch—Mrs. Henderson is expecting you—while the clerk is clearing your things through customs. Then you can plan the shopping. It's hot, but there's usually a sea breeze in the afternoon. It has to be done anyway."

The party divided in three ways after lunch, when Mr. Henderson explained what they had to shop for. He said the cork helmets they bought in Port Said, for protection against the Indian sun, were all right, though there were some who held it wasn't necessary and that only dark glasses were of any real use.

"The helmets will be good to start with, anyway, until you find what is best for each. But there isn't any argument about mosquitoes. You'll need nets for your beds right away when you get to Rajahpur, and there won't be time then to have them made. Buy now and be safe from malaria. That's what we tell everybody. For the train now and for any later traveling you do, a bedding roll is a must. Our trains here are different from those at home. The berths aren't made up. You have to carry your bedding with you."

Barby's watch wouldn't run and Mugsy's glasses needed to be straightened, so they went with Martha to attend to those things. Mr. Henderson went along to help Martha get at the heavy luggage before it was put on the train. She wanted to take out some blankets for the journey up country. Though so warm here in Bombay in the daytime, it was chilly at night this time of year the farther north one went.

Mr. Tennant begged to be excused from any shopping when he found there was a chance to have an interview with a famous Indian lawyer who had risen from the low caste people to be one of the country's respected leaders. He was known to have firm views on religion. It would be worth the whole trip just to meet him.

The boys and their mother penetrated the depths of Crawford Market with Mrs. Henderson, looking for the bedding rolls and nets.

The market was a fascinating place, like an enormous department store with dirt floor and open sides. There were strange fruits they had never heard of in the beautifully arranged displays—custard apples, huge loose-skinned oranges from Nagpur, and horrible-smelling jack fruit.

There were carpets and shirts and toys and cooking things, and one stall had nothing but bright-colored glass bracelets for girls and women to wear in rows on each arm. The owners of the stalls shouted at Mrs. Henderson to bring her guests to them. They sounded like the barkers in side shows at county fairs at home.

Mrs. Henderson said, "They all know me. I bring so many Americans here during a year's time."

It was disappointing that they couldn't stay long after the necessary purchases were made. Mrs. Henderson was apologetic but firm.

"By the time we finish our shopping and get back to the house, there will just be time for dinner and you will have to be off again to the station. Everybody feels the same way when they first come to Bombay and to Crawford Market. They want to look and look and look. For my part, I'd rather take you for a long drive, instead of attending to these dull needs. You really should see Bombay from the top of Malabar Hill and have a

run along the ocean front. Maybe we can do that when you are here next year, going home."

But going home seemed a long way off. They had only just come.

When they came out of the market, the evening mist was beginning to come in from the ocean and the light from the lowering sun tinted it a delicate pink. There was sound, too, everywhere, like a continuous hum from a vast choir, though there were discords in it. The cries of street vendors and beggars were part of it and a sound of singing.

Eve said, "I'd like a record of this. If one could listen to it many times, a pattern would appear, I'm sure, like the notes on a scale or a bar of music."

Mrs. Henderson said, "It sounds pretty awful to me sometimes, especially when there is a street fight added to the beggars. Do you realize why you notice it?"

"No," said Eve, a bit wonderingly. "Is there a special reason why I should?"

"I think so," said their hostess. "It's because the sounds are mostly human. You do hear motor horns, of course, and the policemen's whistles. But if you think of it, the sounds in American city streets are more mechanical than human. Listen again and see if you don't agree."

There was a silence in the car while Eve listened and the boys did, too, and it was broken only when the Henderson driver, with a jerk at the wheel, swerved the car just in time to keep from running over a little beggar boy. He stopped and stormed at the child in rapid, shrill vernacular, and all the people round, who had seen, crowded close and began to discuss it with him. They told each other the same tale over and over, shifting the blame with each recital.

Eve said, "I do see what you mean, but I'm glad the child wasn't hurt."

"He's used to traffic. He didn't even look scared," said Mrs.

Henderson. She spoke to the driver, bidding him start on, and the crowd good-naturedly parted to let the car through.

They found that Martha and the girls had returned ahead of them, and Martha immediately took charge of the new bedding rolls, spreading them out on the cool polished cement floor of the Hendersons' guest room.

The rolls were made of green canvas, waterproofed, with a pocket folded over and stitched at each end. All the edges were bound with leather. There were side flaps to hold the bedding securely inside when rolled up for carrying. It would hold a narrow thin mattress and still roll up compactly.

The Jays fell to and helped Martha count out the blankets and the sheets for each one and roll them up and buckle the straps. The three were still at the job when Mr. Henderson came to say that dinner was ready. He helped fasten the last roll.

"They look a bit slim now," he said, "but wait until you've done some real traveling about India. A bedding roll is the best carryall ever invented. You put into it everything that there isn't room for in the rest of your luggage, and all the extras you buy on the trip. I stuff books in mine and extra shoes and my laundry. It's great."

The rising moon had changed the pink mists to pearl, and there was a damp feeling in the air when they came out to the waiting taxis to go to the station. There the man who had cleared their things through customs was waiting with their train reservations.

There wasn't much time, as Mrs. Henderson had predicted— just enough for the usual thank-yous and good-bys—before the warning whistle made everyone draw his head inside his window like a turtle into its shell. Carriage doors banged all along the platform and then they were moving, out of Bombay, on the last lap of their long journey to Rajahpur.

Lying in his berth in the train later, James tried to remember everything that had happened that day so they could put it in the red book as soon as possible. There hadn't been a moment since leaving the ship to think about Miss Williams's wishes, much less make any attempt to carry them out. He raised himself on one elbow to look around.

An Indian train was an interesting thing by itself, aside from the people who traveled. Each carriage was entered from the station platform, and there was no way to go from one to another inside. Second-class compartments such as they were in had four berths each.

The girls and their mother and Martha had one to themselves. In the one next to it, the Jays had the uppers and their father and an Indian gentleman who was going to Delhi had the lower ones. And they weren't a bit like the closed-in-by-curtains ones in American Pullmans.

The lower berths were two long seats, running the length of the carriage, cushioned in shiny black leather. Above, a shelf similarly cushioned swung by stout chains and leather straps.

In the daytime the travelers from upper and lower berths sat together below and the luggage was stored away above. At night the bedding rolls were unstrapped and spread out flat on the leather cushions. Presto, four beds.

Moonlight lay dimly on the floor of the carriage. A blue electric bulb made a small shadow above the washroom door. James lay down again. He felt lonely to be the only one awake. It was strange that he didn't feel sleepy. It had been a tiring, exciting, and crowded day.

The scene on the deck when they were landing came back, and he remembered his mother's look of dismay when Mr. Henderson mentioned the concert artist business. When had that been and why did she mind if the family knew? They had barely known their mother's maiden name because her parents had died so long ago and there were no Carmichael grandparents therefore. If she had been good enough for concerts—and everyone in Jersey whom they knew said she was a fine musician—why had she given it up? Surely not just to be their mother? She hadn't said a word that anyone knew about when she had to give up her classes in the music school in the seminary, to come on this journey. Barby had been the only one, really, who had made any fuss at all, out loud.

A family went where the father's work was, of course. But if one of the family was good enough to be a concert violinist, what then? Yet here they were, about to live in a strange country for a year so that his father could study how some people long ago had worshiped and what they believed in. What difference would that make in the way people believed now? He remembered asking Martha about that same question one day on the boat.

Martha hadn't hesitated. She said, "Near as I can make out, everything we learn helps us, or it helps somebody else because we know it. We don't keep it to ourselves even when we think we do. It shows in lots of little ways. And the more you know about them, ancient people, I mean, the more you understand other people, but there's some that don't want to understand anything but their own way, and I could name one."

"I could name one, too," said James. "And that's Bill Evans, that boy in our school. Jay and I had to fight him. He isn't so bad now, not with us. He lets us say what we think. I mean he did. We aren't there now. I keep forgetting."

Martha nodded and smiled. "I don't hold with fighting, but I guess boys have to do some by way of growing up. Your father did a good job of that, growing up, I mean. He's the kind understands how other people think. Maybe it's natural that he should take up this kind of study he's doing."

James grinned in the dark. Maybe Martha was right. But she hadn't explained a lot of things in that conversation that she might have. For one thing, why was she so fiercely loyal to their father? And how did she know so much about the kind of growing up he had done? Was he her son? Could Martha be their grandmother and it be necessary to keep it a secret? No, that was silly.

The clang of crossing signals interrupted James's thoughts, and the train rumbled over other tracks and slowed. He leaned on his elbow again to look out and saw that they were stopping at a big station where everything was as active and noisy as the streets of Bombay had been in the daytime.

He threw his covers back and scrambled down from his shelf to sit on the foot of his father's berth and watch the crowds through the open upper half of the carriage door. It had begun to turn cool, as Mr. Henderson had said it would, and he shivered a little, but he would not climb back up for his robe, for fear of missing something.

People were rushing frantically up and down the platform, hunting a place in the train. Babies cried and coolies shouted and struggled with luggage. A man with a tray full of little red clay cups and a brass kettle in his hand went by calling something in a monotonous chant.

"*Cha . . . garm, garm . . . cha,*" he said, over and over again, spreading the words apart and swallowing the g's.

James was conscious of a new odor, and he began sniffing to see if he could tell what it was. It was several things, he decided, a thick mixture of flower fragrance, spices, frying food, orange peeling, smoke, washroom chemicals, and people. Deep inside him there stirred a feeling that he was really beginning to see India outside there and John should be down here sharing it with him. He himself must have been numb all day, not to have felt like this when he was part of the crowd in Bombay. An involuntary breath that seemed to come up from his feet made him want to shout, "We're here. This is it. And we're going to be part of this strange, beautiful land."

It was beautiful. There was color everywhere—in the people's clothing, the tinted air at sunset in Bombay, the flaring torch on the cart of the fried-foods man opposite his window, the moonlight on the dark jungle, which only he had seen this night.

A voice said, low, "This is new to you, I think?"

He looked round. In the light from the platform, he could see the Indian gentleman sitting up in his place and smiling. He had spoken in English.

"Oh yes, sir," said James. "We just came on a boat today."

"That is good," said the man. "I hope you like my country. You want to know what that vender was saying? He has hot tea and he is telling the people. *Garm* is the word for hot."

"Thank you," said James. "I'm not 'garm' now."

The man laughed, and outside the guard shouted and the noise became louder and the voices more shrill. Carriage doors began slamming all along the train. Then the engineer whistled, the guard answered, and the train jerked, backed a little, and then lunged forward and they were away again, pounding north to Delhi. Beyond it a little way would be Rajahpur. Home!

James climbed back to his bed. It was odd to be calling Rajahpur home when they hadn't yet seen it, he thought, before he finally fell asleep, clutching one of the buckles of his bedding roll.

The family met the next day for meals, stepping down to the platform of a station and walking along to the restaurant car, where they rode after they had eaten, until another stop—long enough for them to scramble back to their places—was made.

Barby fussed about the dirt and the wind and said she didn't like the sound of the language. Why didn't everybody speak English? It would be so much more sensible.

"Not for some of these," said Eve gently. "You will realize later, dear, that some of these people can't write their names or read their own written language. This learning business works both ways. You have the greater advantage. It is for you to be gracious and learn theirs."

At lunch the Jays aired what the Indian gentleman had been teaching them all morning and said they were ready now to help Barby. But she would have none of it. "It sounds awful," she said.

No one seemed to connect the boys' new knowledge with Mugsy's determination to stay with her father for the afternoon, so everybody was much surprised at teatime when she told the waiter what she wanted in a good though short vernacular sentence. They had invited the Indian gentleman to join them, and he looked pleased with Mugsy's effort. Barby stared out of the window and took no part in the chatter.

The minaret of a mosque they had been told to watch for as a landmark for Rajahpur came in sight shortly before ten on the second morning. The train slowed and the usual clamor rose. This time the Tennants were a part of the scene. Coolies came swarming, shouting, "I take it, Sahib, the luggage."

The Jays looked at each other. Now was the time. Their Indian friend had said if they spoke even a few words in Hindustani, the coolies would respect them and there would be no trouble getting off the train.

James nodded and John said briskly, *"Acchha, lejao, das chiz,"* meaning, "Very well, take ten things."

One of the men grinned and thrust open the carriage door. *"Hah,"* he said, which meant he understood them. *"Bahut acchha, Chhota Sahib."* And then he came inside the carriage and began tossing their things out to others on the outside. When it was all pitched out, bedding rolls thrown about like footballs, he said, "You speaking very good."

Nearly everything was collected in a heap again, as it had been on the deck of the ship three mornings past, when they heard another strange American voice say, "Oh, here they are,

I'm sure." A tall man in a khaki-colored sun helmet came toward them with outstretched hand.

"Are you Tennant?" he asked. "I'm Roberts, the superintendent of the mission here. We've two cars outside the barrier. Did you have a good journey up?"

The coolies put the bedding rolls and suitcases on top of their heads, and the family followed the long procession to the cars. The trunks in the luggage van would come later on a cart, Mr. Roberts explained. He showed them the sort of cart it would be, a *tela*, a long affair balanced on two wheels, without sides, and manned by several coolies. They would tie the things on with ropes.

The way to the mission compound led along roads shaded by enormous trees, through cantonments where troops were quartered, past the buildings of the Muslim University. Just beyond a large polo ground, the cars turned in at a gate set between low stone walls. There were singing children on either side of the red earth driveway that led to a large white plaster bungalow.

People were gathered on the house steps and the wide, pillared veranda. Many of them carried flower garlands, which they flung round the necks of all the family. Then there were speeches, and a big bouquet of pink roses was presented to Eve. A tiny boy and girl staggered up, each holding the side of a top-heavy white banner, which said WELCOME in golden letters. Their little faces were grave and anxious, and if Martha hadn't grasped Mugsy just in time, she would have darted out to help them with their burden.

Then the boys and girls marched away to their schools again and the Tennants were invited inside the house. This was the one they would live in.

Mrs. Roberts said she would take Mrs. Tennant around and show her everything.

"We didn't do any color washing because we thought you'd like to choose your own tints."

"Color washing!" Eve Tennant echoed questioningly. "I'm afraid I don't understand."

"For the walls. Whitewashing it is, really, but we put a colored powder in and it makes so much difference in a room. You'll see. There are some, of course, who like all white, would never think of tinting. But . . ." She dismissed such people with a wave of her hand and opened the front door.

The children followed the grownups because that seemed to be expected.

"Mother better choose colors. All white isn't the thing, definitely," John whispered, and Barby giggled. Her father turned around and shook his head violently, but they could see he wanted to laugh, too.

They entered a large room directly from the porch. It had a dreary look. On the floor was spread a thick matting woven of what looked like brown string, the kind that came on book parcels at home. In the middle of the high ceiling a large electric fan with three white chipped blades was suspended. There was a fireplace without kindling in the wall opposite the front door, and on either side of it arched niches, waist-high, were shelved with stone slabs but held no books.

A battered, scratched baby-grand piano stood on the left beside a gaping inner doorway. Dr. Tennant stepped away from the group and struck a chord, and the resulting jangle of sound was awful. Barbara put her hands over her ears. "Father, please," she said.

Mr. Roberts saw her. He turned back to them, smiling. "Bad, eh? You have to keep after a piano in this climate. We'll get a man up here, if you think you'll use it. The other folks didn't play it much, but they did hope you wouldn't mind keeping it for them for a while."

"Nobody could use it in this state," said Dr. Tennant, "but we shall want it, decidedly, so please do get your man after it. If the felts are gone, it will take a while."

"Probably I can attend to it next month," said Mr. Roberts. "Awful lot going on right now. I'm pretty busy."

Mugsy said, "Oh, but next month won't be in time for Christmas, and we'll need it then. We always have carols at that time of year."

Mr. Roberts looked down at her, and a slow grin spread over his face. "Well, little Miss America, we'll have to do something about that. Here's my hand on it." He reached and grasped hers. "I don't sing myself, but if you want to sing, then that piano must be fixed."

He stepped to the door and said something to his driver, which no one understood because he spoke so fast, but they knew what it was the driver answered. He said, *"Acchha, Sahib, jaldy."* Jaldy was the word for quickly.

Beyond the shelves on one side, farthest from the piano, another wide, gaping doorway led to a large room behind the fireplace wall.

"This is the dining room," said Mrs. Roberts, starting through. "It opens onto the back veranda. Your pantry is out there, and the cookhouse only a few steps down that path through the kitchen garden. We'll go out there presently."

Barbara made a face and muttered, "Horrible place. I've seen enough, haven't you? It will take an army to make it look like anything. C'mon. Let's get some fresh air."

But air wasn't what she really wanted. They had come a long way to this new home, and if it didn't have what they most hoped for—a substitute for their willow tree—the whole venture would be a total loss. Nothing else would matter, white walls or colored, tuneless, useless piano or a tuned one, nothing.

There were flowers everywhere. Across the roof of the porte-cochere, which sheltered people getting out of cars and tongas in the rainy season, a thick antigonum vine sprawled its heart-shaped leaves and masses of delicate pink bloom.

Roses filled the plot between the side of the house and the hedge along the road. They were trained up trellises and covered a small arbor, which opened on the back garden. Sweet peas in racks edged a tennis lawn.

But the flowers were not important, not that day.

The children circled the house and found another wide porch on the opposite side, and in a small room opening onto it their father and Mr. Roberts were sitting talking. It looked like a library or small office.

A line of tall trees led along a dirt driveway to another bungalow beyond. The grass was littered with their large, dried leaves.

Then John gave a piercing whistle, and said "I spy," and took off at a run with the others at his heels. He was headed toward a far corner of the garden beyond the cookhouse. They found a gardener at work in a shed there, potting chrysanthemums.

The feathery canes of a stand of bamboo that screened the shed had fooled John, and he had thought it was willow, their search ended.

The gardener stopped work and beamed at them, but they didn't notice him. Barby looked at the boys, and their faces were solemn. They had seen everything in the garden now, and there wasn't a willow tree anywhere. It had to be in their own compound to do any good. Barby seemed ready to cry.

Before the others could catch their breath, Mugsy said, "Oh, pooh, it doesn't matter, not very much. We can do a lot of other things. Look at all those children I'll have to play with. And we've got a whole year to do everything. Come on. We're to go to the Robertses' for lunch, I heard them say, and they'll wonder where we are. I'm hungry."

No one else was, but they followed her back to the house.

7: CHRISTMAS PROGRAM

New people went to call on those already living in a place, it seemed, instead of the other way around, as at home. So the Tennant parents, accompanied by Mrs. Roberts and occasionally by Margaret Stanton, principal of the girls' school, spent their first few days in Rajahpur meeting the school staff and station officials.

The children were content to stay at home because the color-washing job had begun. They watched the process in astonishment and got in the way and asked questions.

A room had to be prepared properly before the whitewash was applied. The matting was taken up, showing brick floors beneath. All the furniture was put on the veranda, and the helpers brought in earth that was carefully spread on the floor. Then the ladders and the buckets came in and the delicate tints were mixed and applied with brushes made of lengths of heavy bamboo, pounded at the ends until the fibres separated into usable bristles.

The necessity for the layer of dirt on the floor became apparent when the work began. It was meant to catch the generous spatters from the coarse brushes and so keep the bricks clean. It was vastly cheaper than using the tarpaulins spread down by painters at home.

When a wall dried, the dirt was swept out and the matting relaid, so that the furniture could be brought in again.

On the second day the piano tuner appeared, but he did not seem to mind the confusion all about him and tapped away happily until he was satisfied.

It was a confused week, their first one in the house behind the antigonum vine. Each member of the family was learning something. A few of the lessons were painful, but there was laughter, too.

Dr. and Mrs. Tennant had begun studying Hindustani at once, determined to speak it as quickly as possible, though Ram Gopal, the houseman, and the old cook both knew some English.

Everybody laughed the day Mrs. Tennant tried to order new mattresses and found that she had really said she wanted a donkey.

The red book told the story of the children's disappointment about the willow tree.

From the Book of the Jays   Rajahpur, Dec. 5

We came here today. There is no willow tree in this garden. They say we will have to go to Kashmir to see those. It is more than seeing. They do not understand, but Mother and Father do. They talked to us. Mother said, "It isn't the house and it isn't what you have in it or around it that makes a home. It is being with the people you like best in a good place."

We haven't decided yet if this is a good place. But Mother knows what we did under our willow tree in America—talked and kept our things in the old cupboard. And nobody came there unless we asked them. She said that part was wrong. But maybe there won't be much time to be alone here, anyway. From the talk, it seems that mission people, the mothers and children anyway, move around a lot on account of school and rains. We are to stay here until March and then go up to the American school in the hills. Jay says he doesn't mind too much about the tree. Barby cares most. She doesn't like anything here yet.

James Tennant

No donkeys were brought and the new mattresses were made on the front veranda. First a huge pile of raw cotton was flicked

by hand into clean, seedless rolls, called batts. The rhythmic twanging of the carding bow went on most of one day. Then a tailor came and sat on a cotton rug in front of a small sewing machine, which he operated by turning the wheel with his right hand. He stitched the ticking cases for the mattresses, and when they were ready, he spread the cotton on each one and rolled it in.

A boy who was learning tailoring in the school was called to sew the ends together and tie each mattress in a tight diamond pattern so the cotton would not slide around.

That was how the Jays first met Dhayan Singh.

He was taller than they but looked to be about the same age. His feet were bare, but a pair of shoes that looked too large for him was set carefully out of the way against the house wall. He had stepped out of them on arrival, as was the custom. An old jacket was neatly folded by the shoes. His khaki shirt and trousers were clean but faded almost white from many washings.

When the Jays appeared, he gave them a quick gesture of greeting, a hand at his forehead, and went on with his work, his long, thin fingers thrusting the large needle through the heavy cloth in sure motions.

The boys were on their way into the house. "Sewing!" said John. "I thought women did that."

"Everything's turned around here. To our way. Theirs probably seems all right to them. The men cook, too," James answered. "You forget His Royal Highness in our kitchen."

"Which reminds me what we came in for, something to eat."

"It's you that's hungry. You can't be, though, after that breakfast you ate. And not an hour ago. Besides, can we get anything this time of day?"

"We can if we find Mother and the keys. Or Martha."

"Martha, more likely. Listen! She's got something else—trouble, maybe?"

There was a loud discussion being held somewhere in the

back precincts. The boys followed the sound of voices through to the rear porch.

Martha had a cake in progress at a wooden table opposite the door. Mugsy and her ayah, an Indian woman in full white skirt, waist, and head scarf, stood together watching. Mugsy's eyes were shining and her helmet hung round her neck by its chin strap. Her hands were full of limp roses.

The cook, Hyder Khan, a tall old man with a deep voice behind a handsome square-cut beard, was measuring flour. Ram Gopal was beating egg whites. Around Martha's mixing bowl was a strange assortment of spices in little ragged bits of newspaper, a lump of pink rock salt, and a row of fluted cup-cake forms.

The flour was whirling.

Martha said, "I only want to help you, Hyder Khan, so that you can do it properly next time."

He snorted, almost. His voice rose. He said, "Properly! What is properly? Your way or mine? My way is good; it was good enough before you came. All things I know so well I threw my rule book away."

Martha stopped the mixing. "Didn't your book say anything about keeping spices neatly in tins so they would not lose strength? And salt? This way it isn't clean. And the flour tied in a cloth!"

The cook banged the flour sifter on the table. He said, "I, then, am going. Now. I will tell the Mem. I cannot please you. Let another learn your way."

He marched off, and there was a moment of complete silence on the back porch. It allowed them to hear the deep throb of Eve's violin, coming from inside. Her morning practice was beginning. She had time for it because Martha had come to India with them. But if the servants left because of Martha's bossiness, what then? Maybe they could head him off and explain that Martha was really only trying to teach him better ways.

Martha said, "Oh, bother," and began to sift the flour.

Ram Gopal saw the Jays disappearing in the doorway, following the cook, and Mugsy and the ayah after them. The egg beater stopped. If there was going to be a really big row, he didn't intend to miss the show.

But there was only a room full of people listening to the woman playing, on a thing something like an Indian *zithar*, though she was holding it under her chin instead of on her knees. Ram Gopal had never seen its like before, and he stayed to listen. That Miss Sahib could beat the eggs herself.

From the Book of the Jays   Rajahpur
                                                   December 11

We had a sort of concert this morning. Martha and the cook got in a row over a cake, and he was firing himself. He was impudent to Martha. She was only trying to teach him something. But she was sort of abrupt and didn't lead up to it beforehand, which you have to do here. It's their way.

Mother was starting to practice, and Hyder Khan barged right into the drawing room and we after him to help Mother. But we didn't have to. All the people from the house were coming in. The tailor and that boy from the school sat inside the doorway. Mugsy and the ayah got the cook between them by the fireplace. Mother kept on playing. When Ram Gopal stuck his head in the door, we motioned him to join the crowd.

Father came out of his study and one of the masters in there with him came too. The people who lived here before us left their piano. It had to be tuned, and it was a good thing they got after it right away. Father sat down to play for Mother, the way he used to do at home, and they didn't stop for maybe half an hour.

When it was over, the cook got up, made Mother a deep bow, and marched back to his kitchen. That's in a little house by itself behind ours. He was still here at dinner time tonight. We had a swell cake for lunch. And there was curry for dinner. Martha made it but he showed her how.

John Tennant

From the Book of the Jays December 11
(John hasn't written enough today.)

Mugsy has got an ayah. We have not explained that before. That is a person like a nurse, mostly for babies. Martha says Mugsy is big enough to look after herself. But practically every house in India has one, if you need her or not, it seems. Mugsy's is named Sherbatti. You can't tell how old she is. She wears a lot of thin silver bracelets on her arms and two thick ones on her ankles and a ring on one toe that Barby tried to buy, without any luck. She jingles, the ayah, not Barby, all the time. It sounds pretty, a sort of music, like the high notes Mother plays.

Ayahs know how to do an awful lot of things. Sherbatti washes our socks and would make our beds, but Mother won't let her. She says we have to do our own. Dhayan Singh does his. That is the boy from the school who sewed the mattresses. He is learning tailoring. His teeth haven't any holes. He has never been to a dentist. He chews charcoal and brushes his teeth with a pounded-up end of a twig. It works. We have tried it.

James Tennant

From the Book of the Jays December 12

There is something new to write in this book every day. Celia Roberts came home today. She is a little older than Barby. There are no boys in the Roberts family. Not here. Only that girl. She laughs a lot. She has been in the hills at the school where we are supposed to go when it begins again in March. It is too cold up there now to have school. That is why Celia is here. Everything is "keen" with her. She's got Barby saying it already.

Dhayan Singh says his school will have a holiday next week until after Christmas. He will stay here because his home vil-

lage is too far away. He is wild about Mother's music. He talks
about it a lot and asks so many questions. We can't answer half
he wants to know. We've been going to the school playing field
to watch games in the afternoons. These boys do a lot of hockey.

John Tennant

The Jays were restless during school hours when Dhayan and
the others were still at lessons. Everyone else had something to
do.

Barby spent hours giggling about nothing with Celia Roberts.

Mugsy had begged to sit in class with a new friend at the
girls' school, Charity Abide they called it, from an old verse on
its gatepost. The new friend's name was Sajida, granddaughter
of the Tennants' cook.

"She can speak to me," said Mugsy, already proud of her
friend's abilities. "She learns it in the class."

"Aren't you going to learn to speak to her?" Mrs. Tennant
asked. "You made a good start in the train."

"Too much bother for only a year," said Barbara.

"Anything one knows is useful," Martha reproved her. "I'm
going to take some lessons in this Hindustani, too."

"You!" the family chorused.

"Why not? Miss Stanton says you never know when you
might need it."

So, after breakfast each day it became the family habit to
separate to its various interests, all but the Jays who had nothing
to do. One morning they drifted out onto the back veranda,
watching Ram Gopal clear away. He was using the lower steps
of the stairway to the roof for temporary shelves for plates while
he scrubbed the table.

"We haven't been topside yet. Let's see what we can see."

Ram Gopal moved the plates patiently, and they climbed.
An extra room had been added on the flat roof for sleeping in

the hot weather or the rainy season. A pierced stone balustrade, waist-high, rose around the roof edge, so that one could walk there as if on the deck of a ship. The roof was a good lookout over the whole mission, like a little town spread out below them, except that there were no shops.

Beyond the two family bungalows the buildings of the boys' school were reached by a branch of the main driveway. Grouped together, there were the schoolhouse, the masters' houses, the dormitories, the eating shed and kitchen, and the storerooms. The boys' playing field lay farther on at the back, shaded by ancient trees.

Facing the town road was the small, pleasant bungalow where Fitz would one day live. On its other side, across a narrow lane, was the girls' school and all its buildings.

The sounds of people at work came up to the roof and the fragrances from the garden and the freshly dampened driveway. The sun was warm, and it would soon be lunchtime. But the Jays had no part in the program here at Rajahpur. They turned away listlessly and were going downstairs again when James said, "I wonder what is inside the room. It doesn't seem that we are going to use it, does it?"

It didn't look as if anyone had used it in a long time. The doors, wooden below and glass above, needed painting. They were made in pairs that fastened in the middle, making a wide opening for lifting beds in and out easily.

John opened the nearest pair to make their survey and heard a faint clicking sound at the same time that something cold touched his neck. He yelled and brushed frantically at the place. A small grayish green lizard, called a *chipkalli*, fell with a smack at his feet. It lay so still that only the fluttering of its throat showed it was alive.

"How can anything living be so cold? It's a horrible feeling to have it touch you." John rubbed the back of his neck.

"It's more scared than you were," said James. "Look!" When he moved to pick it up, it darted across the doorsill and was gone.

"Ugh!" said John. "Let's get out of here."

James put his head in the door before he closed it. "Full of old things," he reported. "Hi, Jay, here's an old deck chair. Maybe we could fix it up."

"Come *on*," said John, from the top step. "I don't want anything to do with it. It's probably full of lizards."

Downstairs the place began to look less dreary every day. Mrs. Tennant and the tailor and Dhayan Singh, after school, were making curtains for all the doorways. The bare look of the high-ceilinged rooms was disappearing. The furniture had been polished and the plain chests and teakwood tables lost their heaviness against the lovely colors in chintz and walls.

The professor refused curtains for the study, the little room at the right of the drawing room as one came in. "This is a man's room," he said stoutly. "The schoolboys and the masters will be coming to see me here often. No frills for us."

Off the dining room was a small room that shared the office porch. The Jays had been sleeping there. "It will be just until you go to the hills," said their mother. "Then I'll make a little office out of it for me. I need a place where the cook can bring his accounts and where I can write letters."

That plan needed some discussion. "Looks to me like we won't belong much anywhere," said John. "We'd have been better off if we had asked Mother to let us stay in Jersey. School in the spring, to live in a dorm probably, and no room of our own when we come back here."

"We won't stay long when we do return," said James. "It will be going home time then. A year from now. Remember?"

John snapped his fingers. "Ah! Keen! Aw, no, I mean swell. That girl!"

After lunch they wandered out across the lawns to watch the

oxen drawing water from Miss Stanton's well to irrigate the girls' vegetable garden. They were beautiful white gentle-eyed beasts, and they each wore a necklace of large blue beads. The well man was singing when the boys arrived, the song they had heard when they first came to Rajahpur, a phrase repeated again and again. The measure was a guide for the animals and amusement for the man all in one, something about the water coming up and the empty bucket, an enormous skin hooked to the sweep, going down again.

There was a group of small yellow banana trees, the kind called plantains, around the well. A long line of poinsettias with heavy bloom heads taller than Barby separated the well from a tennis lawn. It seemed odd that with all the greenness and color everywhere it should be so cold at night when the sun was gone. Then all the house doors were shut and fires laid in the grates.

Miss Stanton had a carpenter who lived on the place and made things for the whole mission. There was always a wonderful smell of fresh shavings and oil and polish about the little lean-to where he worked. He was a quiet man with skilled hands, and he grinned at the boys when they stopped in their wandering to talk to him. They could admire what he was making without saying the words. Today he seemed to be putting a bookcase together. He had a shelf board in his vise, sandpapering it smooth. The wood had a beautiful grain, and when he pointed to the tree that shaded his lean-to, they knew he meant it was teak.

One Saturday morning, after another purposeless excursion around the compounds—all the boys were busy with Saturday duties, so there was no luck there—the Jays carried deck chairs to the deserted brick terrace in front of the empty house that would be Fitz's some day. It was peaceful there. Bees hummed in the roses. The bells of a *tonga*, India's two-wheeled horse-drawn taxi, sounded from the highway. Some coolies went by, chanting a queer tune to which they kept step. They were carrying the top of a large table on their heads, and the detached legs rolled around on it as they moved.

When these sounds died away, there was only the bees' hum until Mugsy and the ayah came along the drive from Miss Stanton's house. Mugsy held up a square white envelope.

"An invitation," she said. "We took a note for Mother, and Miss Stanton gave me this."

"Who's it for?"

"All of us, for a program."

The Jays pretended to be bored. They groaned realistically, and John said, "You go; we're too tired. You can tell us about it."

But they were on hand the night of the twenty-second. It was the usual school closing affair before Christmas vacation. The assembly hall was almost full when the Tennant family arrived.

The boys' school had been invited, too. Some of them had sisters there. They sat at one side and the girls on the other. The back was filled with the compound families. Ram Gopal stood about, holding his little baby. He wore a pale blue turban, and a bright pink waistcoat showed under his jacket. He had on his best things.

Everyone was talking, and the buzz grew a little louder when Miss Stanton took the Tennants up to a front bench. Those were the seats of high honor in India, they learned.

When they were settled, Dr. Tennant looked along the row. "Where's Mugsy?" he whispered loudly. "Didn't she come? She could stay up late one night, couldn't she?"

"Shsh! It's all right. Look, they're going to begin."

The curtains drew apart and the talking stopped. It was the old, old scene, much the same as they might have looked at on this holiday night in their own suburban church, nine thousand miles away.

Up to that moment the Jays hadn't thought much about Christmas. There had been nothing here except perhaps the poinsettias to remind them of the great festival. Now in front of them were the shepherds and the star. A wobbly one it was, on a wire they could plainly see. But it stood for all the things they'd miss this year.

John whispered, "I say, Jay, have you thought about any presents? You got any money?"

"Shsh!" said their mother.

James could only shake his head, and his meaning wasn't clear. He could have thoughts and no money, or neither one. John fidgeted.

Then the curtains closed and a group of little girls appeared in front of it. "These are our day pupils," said Miss Stanton. "They have come to sing for us."

It took the Tennants a few seconds to discover Mugsy, standing by Sajida at the end of the line. No wonder they hadn't

seen her sooner. The small full Muslim trousers she wore and
the blouse and filmy head scarf were exactly like Sajida's. And
she had the ayah's bracelets, though obliged to keep her fist
doubled to make them stay on. They jingled satisfactorily when
she raised her hand to pull the sliding scarf back on her head.

Mugsy was bursting with the success of her surprise. They
could see her struggling to keep her face straight. When the
song began, the family watched her mouth, because the words
were Hindustani, though the tune was an old English favorite.
She seemed to be singing what the others were. It seemed indeed that India had become a good place for the youngest Tennant.

The next evening they were still sitting round the dinner
table, cracking nuts and idling, when Ram Gopal came in with
a note for Dr. Tennant on his tray.

"Hullo, what's this?" said Dr. Tennant.

"Sahib sent it," said Ram Gopal.

Dr. Tennant laid down a walnut deliberately and ripped the
envelope carefully while the family watched. He smiled as he
read, and the smile became broader.

"It's something wonderful. And it doesn't have girls in it.
I can tell," Mugsy exclaimed.

Her father laughed. "Absolutely right the first time, baby.
How did you guess? It sounds like you had the gift of second
sight."

"Then can I go along, because I know, even if I am a girl?"

"You may not."

"Where?" said the Jays together.

"Where would you like to go?"

"Everywhere, Father. We haven't been any place, yet. How
can we tell?"

"Then say hunting," said Mugsy.

"Father! Not really? What for? How does *she* know?"

"Mrs. Roberts wants peafowl for Christmas dinner, so Mr.

Roberts is going out to get her some," said Mugsy. "We're all going to eat together, so we'll have it, too. And I know, account of their ayah said so."

"The reliable Indian grapevine," said her mother. "I've heard of it."

"So that's what ayahs are for. I wondered," said Dr. Tennant.

"But you don't eat peacocks!" John was horrified, remembering the proud strutters on the lawns at Warwick Castle.

"Some people do," said his father. "Listen to this!" He read from the note still in his hand.

> "Dear Tennant:
>
> "If you and the boys care to join me tomorrow morning for a little shooting, I'll be glad to have you. Normally we don't kill peafowl around here. They are a sacred bird to the Hindus, and it causes feeling. But some Christian villagers have sent in word that a flock near them is becoming a menace to the grain crop. We should get a good bag. Roasted peahen is fine eating. You can't tell it from turkey if it is done properly. I'll drive past your house about five."

"Whoops!" said John.

"B-r-r-r," said James. "My teeth are chattering already. It's cold these mornings before the sun comes up." Under cover of the laughter he said, low, to John, "What about taking Dhayan Singh?"

"Excuse me, Eve," said their father, "I'll go along to the study and answer this. All right, boys? Accepting, are you?"

They were excused too and followed him to the office. James didn't wait for John to ask their favor. It was his idea. He said, "Father, if there's room, could anybody else go along?"

"Not Mugsy, certainly, if that's who."

John said, "No, Father, it's a boy. Dhayan Singh. He can't go home for Christmas."

"Who's he?"

"One of the schoolboys. He helped sew on the mattresses."

"Oh, that one. H'm! Too bad to take just one Indian boy when there is a whole class . . ."

"No, Father, only three. Everybody but those three out of sixth class could go home."

Mr. Tennant had started to write his note. He laid down the pen and leaned back in his chair.

"You seem to know a lot about the school. How would . . . ? Never mind. I'll ask you that later. I daresay it would be all right to add another boy, if Roberts doesn't object. I'll go along over there and see, instead of writing an answer. If he goes, the boy should sleep here tonight, so we shan't be delayed in the morning."

It was as good as done, the Jays knew, and they went off to work on stamps until bedtime.

8: A BAG OF PEAFOWL

The moon in its last quarter was still visible when the Robertses' car rolled in under the pink vine next morning at five. Light shone faintly from the rear of the house, and presently the front door opened and Mr. Tennant and the three boys appeared. They were trying to be quiet, but their excited whispering seemed loud in the still, damp air of dawn.

"We haven't far to go, but we must get there before it's too light, so we can see where the peafowl fly to feed from their home tree," Mr. Roberts explained. "You sit with me, Tennant. The boys can have the back seat to themselves. Captain Meredith lent me a gun for you. He's the head of the police here. What's that you have?"

The professor held up a shapeless carryall bag. "Coffee!" he said. "A thermos full. Mrs. Tennant's idea. We've brought enough cups in our pockets."

"Excellent. This chill gets inside a man before he knows it."

They had smooth going out of town and until they reached the track across the fields to the village. After that they bumped over cart ruts for a couple of miles, until a faint promise of sunrise joined to the light from a tiny slice of moon low in the west showed them Minapur village just ahead.

Mist wreaths rolling along the ground looked like smoke when the car stopped. And their breath seemed an extension of the mist, puffing out of their mouths with each word spoken. The boys followed the two men, and the smell of the village came to them on the dawn wind. James sniffed. This was different from the railway platform, but it was India, too.

There were many mud houses forming the village, with
thatch for roofs, built solidly together and reached by crooked
lanes that stemmed away from a large open space that had a
well in the center. In a clump of trees not far from the well,
Mr. Roberts pointed out the vague, lumpy shadows of peacocks
roosting.

"Come," he said. "We will let the *padre* know we are here,"
and he led the way along one of the lanes.

There were cattle byres built against some of the houses,
and when he saw those, James knew the essence of the village
smell. It was only another mixture of many parts, fresh milk,

straw, the smoke of cooking fires beginning to puff out of low doorways, and cow-dung cakes drying for fuel on house walls.

A few people were stirring, early as it was, so the news of their coming sped along ahead of them and the village minister was waiting in his doorway when they approached. He was full of apology.

"If I'd known the day, my wife would have been ready for you. Now there is no tea prepared."

"Never mind, Padre Sahib," said Mr. Roberts. "Tell her not to worry. We've brought coffee with us." He cocked his head. "Ah, listen!"

A raucous screaming sound, harsh and clamorous like the loud mewing of kittens, many times multiplied, came from the trees by the well.

"The birds! There they go."

It had grown lighter, and they could see the peacocks, scudding across the low roofs, tails streaming, toward the fields outside the village.

"They've been in the sugar cane lately," said the minister. "And they're spoiling the wheat. It is bad for everyone."

"We'll fix some of your trouble," said Mr. Roberts, laughing.

They waited a little until the birds settled to their feeding. Once started at that, the hunters could choose their marks and make their shots count.

It was colder in the open, and the hot coffee was welcome. John sat down on the running board of the old car and warmed his hands on his cup. "What would Bill Evans say to this?"

"I can answer that in one guess," said James. "He'd snoot our equipment, car included, and brag about the guns he is going to have when he's twenty-one."

"I certainly don't want to shoot anything," said James slowly, "and we're lucky to be allowed coffee once in a while. Why can't that guy learn to enjoy what he has at the moment?"

John started to say something, but somewhere, far off, a rooster crowed, and he was answered from several directions. The day had come.

When they left the car, far across the fields against the northern sky a faint blue line showed, and Mr. Roberts said they were looking at the first low hills of the Himalayas. "On a clear day," he added, "we can sometimes see a snow peak or two."

John said, "Imagine! The mountains. Bill Evans will have a fit when Miss Williams reads out this part from our book. I can't think of a thing he could drag in that would sound bigger."

Dhayan Singh said, "Book? Is it writing a real book, like our reader in the school?"

"No," said James. He explained.

Dhayan shook his head. "The Americans have too much learning, to teach their children to do such a thing as an extra. More extra. Here, we . . ."

"Shsh!"

Mr. Roberts reached for a gun. A fine bird was changing its feeding place. The boys scarcely breathed. Did he have a chance? The gun cracked and a few disturbed birds flew up. But when they settled again, Dhayan Singh ran to fetch the dead one, which lay a couple of yards away.

Now it might be harder going, with all the flock on edge after that too-early first shot. There was to be no more talking and would the boys take turns staying near the car?

A little later in the morning James and his father were separated from the others in a far field.

"I've just one more shell," said Mr. Tennant. "Let's do a little teamwork. There's a big cock feeding in this grain. See how the top of it moves as if a little wind were blowing over it? It stops when the bird stops."

He looked at James critically. "H'm! I hadn't noticed how you've grown these past weeks. This climate is good for you, I guess. I was afraid it mightn't be. Well, since Mugsy isn't here, you'll have to do. Crawl in there and inch along a bit at a time as if you were another peacock feeding behind him. Then flush him up where I can get a good shot. Be ready when I whistle."

James went to earth, feeling suddenly as large as an elephant. He couldn't see the bird, and it seemed a long time until he heard the low signal. He said, "Shoosh!" then, and almost in front of him the peacock soared. He flung himself flat, away from the chance of a misfire, with only his head up to watch the flight. The sun caught the gorgeous color in the wings, shining like silk. When the gun spoke, the color became the cold business of their Christmas dinner.

They did get a good bag, as Mr. Roberts had hoped. After they reached the car, the birds were spread on the edge of the field by the road. They were sorted a little as to weight before they were parceled out. Two for the village *padre,* of course, who would see that a number of hungry souls would be fed.

One for the boys left behind at the school, in Dhayan's mess. Two for the missionary dinner—fourteen people there—and one for the girls at Charity Abide.

Six birds in all. A really good bag for two hunters who were not sportsmen and three boys who had never gone on a peacock shoot before.

They made better time going home because it was daylight, and the Jays saw the country beyond the town. A farmer was plowing a field, using a primitive wooden plow to scratch his furrows. His oxen were thin, gaunt beasts.

"He's late with his plowing," said Mr. Roberts. "We need a good agricultural school, with tractors and teachers to help the farmers try new methods. They are wearing out their topsoil. But change can't come until the Indian himself accepts it. He doesn't accept until he understands, and there aren't enough of us, in mission or in government, to help the understanding."

The sun was high now, almost noon, and the boys rolled down the car windows because they were too warm. The clean smell of the freshly turned earth came in, and the sight of the crows following the farmer's furrow made it seem more like spring or summer at home. But this was the Indian cold weather and in a few hours it would be Christmas Eve.

John remarked that and James said, "And presents still to buy. I'm glad now we didn't think of it before. We can get all Indian things—something different."

"The brass bazaar will be best for you, then," said Mr. Roberts. "I'd offer to take you, but my wife wants the car this afternoon."

"That's all right," said John. "We haven't been in a *tonga* yet."

"May I go with you?" their father asked. "I haven't done my shopping either."

They dropped Dhayan Singh at the school with his bird. He held it carefully by the legs when he lifted his hand in the usual gesture of farewell.

"Curry!" he said, and they all laughed.

9: INDIAN WILLOW

The Jays could almost see their faces, much elongated, in the bright brass trim of the little cart that Ram Gopal called after lunch. The lamp frames and the knobs on the hand railing glittered. Dr. Tennant sat in front with the driver, and the Jays perched on the other seat, facing back.

The rubber-tired wheels went smoothly, and the rhythmic klop, klop of the horse's feet on the hard road mingled with their talking. The Jays were counting the amount of money they had between them and checking their intentions as they rolled along.

Dr. Tennant said, "I could make a suggestion if I were asked."

"We ask you," said John.

"Everything you see will be new to you. Probably you will want to buy the lot. Roberts says this is a very good brass town and that anything we get will be useful at home in showing Indian arts and crafts. Why don't you buy together, one thing for each member of the family from the Jays? You can make an even better choice for your money that way."

They looked at each other. "O.K. Jay?"

"Check."

"O.K., Father."

Christmas Eve in the brass bazaar was only another day's business to the merchants, who sat there behind their bright wares. The *tonga* stopped at the top of the short, narrow street. On both sides of it were brass shops, open in front, set up a few steps from the roadway so that the floor came waist-high to a purchaser on foot.

They got down and as if that were a signal, a loud chorus began. "Buy from me, Sahib; my prices are cheap."

"Come to me; I give you a bargain."

"Nay, my shop is the best, Sahib. All the mission people come here."

Mr. Tennant waved his hand and grinned at them and said, "We'll see all of you, in turn. Come along, boys."

A little crowd gradually gathered around them to watch, as the word sped from shop to shop that the new Americans in the station had come. The crowd was as interested in the shoppers as in the purchases. The Jays were already used to the remarks they heard.

"Two of them."

"Just alike."

"No difference at all."

There was a difference, which the Jays themselves were slow to reveal, ever. The little mole under James's left ear had had its many conveniences. So they only grinned, looked at the brass, and even took the advice the crowd gave.

"Nay, baba," said a tall older boy who carried a pile of books in a strap. "Not that bowl. Take this one."

The shopkeeper frowned, but they chose the smaller, better-fashioned rose bowl for Martha and it was wrapped in a piece of newspaper and handed over to the *tonga* driver to guard.

At the next place they found a tall graceful vase in black enamel and silver on a brass backing. "It would make a fine lamp," said James. "I think Mother will like this."

Their father obligingly delayed a little, and they went on to the next shop. He had business, too, he reminded them.

"Look at the camels, Jay!"

That merchant had nothing but animals it seemed. And he had them in all kinds and sizes. "Made in Jaipur," he said, when they stopped.

"See, there," said James excitedly, "those with the trappings! They're like the ones the Wise Men rode. Let's get a present for the house, too, and put 'em on the mantel. If Martha would make us some Wise Men sometime—to sit on them—check?"

John got the idea at once. They sat down on the shop floor to examine carefully the scarlet and blue enamel trappings of each camel and finally chose three. They were five inches high, and the molder had put reality in the lift of each head. They would stand alone, and it took only a little imagination to see a full-robed figurine in the saddle, guiding the way for the shambling feet.

The boy with the book strap was still with them. He beamed as if he had become personally responsible for their good choices.

"Are these all right?" John asked.

"Very good," he said. "You American?"

John nodded.

"A fine country," said the boy. "It is written here." He touched his books.

John said, "Thank you. I hope you can go there sometime."

"I want to," said the boy. His eyes shone with his anticipation. "Are you going to buy more?"

"What's for Father, Jay?"

"Something for his desk, maybe. It looks kinda bare," said James.

The shopman pointed to the elephants. "Most Sahibs like these," he urged.

"There," said the schoolboy, pointing to a realistic one with hide markings cleverly etched in and a lifted, curling trunk. "It is the sign of good luck when the trunk is up."

"Oh, thank you for the tip," said John. "Let's take it."

The parcels were piling up in the *tonga* and lights were beginning to push the late afternoon shadows back and they had nothing yet for the girls.

"Sisters, is it?" said the schoolboy. "Girls like flowers. Take vases."

They were on the other side of the street now. Dr. Tennant was already there, apparently enjoying a joke with the merchant.

Trays and candlesticks and small boxes were spread out on the white-cotton floor cloth of the shop. They chose candlesticks for Barby's dressing table and a small box with a hinged lid, enameled in pink and purple and green, for Mugsy. Their list was complete and they had spent all their money.

The little horse sped home because he thought there would be food at the end of his road. The Jays did not talk much on the way. They had seen too many things, and now it was dark and they realized that they were strangers in a foreign country on Christmas Eve.

Once James spoke musingly. "I hope Mother has some wrappings. I never thought of those."

"She will," said their father. "She'll think of something."

She had more than wrappings, they found. There was firelight, and tea was laid in the drawing room with the best cloth. And on it one of Martha's chocolate cakes and the cups and plates bought in London were waiting.

Mugsy, dressed in her Muslim finery, opened the door for them.

"We're having Christmas now," she announced. "Right

away. Tea and then the presents. Mother says never mind how they're wrapped. It will be more fun."

It was. They had only time to wash away bazaar dust before Ram Gopal brought in the large family-size teapot that Martha had found in the bazaar the day after their arrival. Their own was too small.

"We went shopping too," said Mugsy. "Mrs. Roberts took us in the car."

"So that's why we had to take a *tonga*," said John. "Women!"

"I only went along to see the fruit market," said their mother. "And it's a wonderful sight. I did most of my Christmas shopping in Port Said."

"Who would think of it there, in that heat?" said John.

"And especially Mother, when she never carries a purse if she can help it."

"Ah, but I was with her," said Martha. "I carried the purse and half her packages."

Mrs. Tennant made a face, but Martha had begun to serve the tea and didn't see it.

The cake disappeared. The litter of torn newspaper mounted. The fireplace received most of it, to make room for the rest. On the mantel the three camels took up their Christmas journeyings with the Tennant family, in front of a row of Christmas cards which had arrived in the last home mail. The largest one was from Fitz on which he had scrawled, "Next Christmas I'll be there." Barby had muttered, "But we won't," and everyone pretended not to hear.

The family liked the camels and Martha promised Wise Men for next year, "wherever we may be."

"Home, of course, Martha, or at least on the way," said Barbara promptly. But no one cheered.

When the pile of things in front of the Jays had all been opened, there was still nothing from their father and mother. The talking had stopped. The family was watching them.

It was an odd silence, and John looked around to see why.

"Oh, I say, Jay," he said. "Here! We missed something. Look!"

He held an envelope, picked up off the floor. It said on the outside, "For the Jays with Christmas greetings from Father and Mother. Your present is on the roof. Go and get it."

There was something hard inside the envelope, and when they opened it, they found a small, ordinary padlock key. What would it open? A new trunk? A big box full of something mysterious? Why would it be on the roof? It was a joke! It must be. They knew what was on the roof. A room full of lizards and old deck chairs.

Their mother saw the doubt growing in their eyes. She said, "It's not a joke, dears. It's real. I'll go with you to see. Come."

Their father followed them out through the back veranda and up the stairs. There was a light in the roof room.

"Try the key, Jays. Your gift is inside."

It was an enormous present. A room of their own. They couldn't take it in, all at once. The hideous storeroom full of junk was gone. It had become a perfect room for boys, for two boys particularly who had thought there was no place at all for them in this house.

The stored things had been removed, everything they would not need. A large dark red cotton rug hid all but the edges of fresh cocoa matting. The beds on opposite sides of the room had spreads with colored stripes that matched the rug. There were identical chests by the beds. Between the two pairs of doors nearest the stairs, shelves had been built with drawers beneath.

In the middle of the room, between the beds was a wide, old-fashioned teakwood desk, polished to show the beautiful grain. It had columns of drawers on both sides.

The Jays had no words at all. Their father, who had been walking about examining things came back to the desk and sat down in one of the chairs there.

Mrs. Tennant looked at him and said, "Your turn now." She perched on the nearer bed.

The Jays stood close together, a little awkwardly, watching. Now what? Wasn't the room enough?

"We had to leave this old desk up here," said Mr. Tennant. He sounded as if he was apologizing for something. "Too heavy to move. It ought to be in a mission museum somewhere. But we thought you might make use of it. That is, we've been thinking . . ."

Mrs. Tennant didn't help him. He cleared his throat and rubbed his hand along the smooth wood. "It was a fine idea. I'm not so sure now—" He glanced at Eve.

She smiled. "Go on. It has to be said."

"I almost asked you this yesterday. How would you like to stay here and go to school with these Indian boys instead of waiting to go to the hills in March?"

"You mean that we wouldn't go to that hill school at all?"

"That's right. We hope you shan't mind too much. Maybe it's a little selfish of us, but we'd like some of our children here."

"Mind, Father! It's the best present you ever gave us."

Something was released inside the Jays. They turned hand-springs and they did a double jig before they remembered to be polite and express their thanks properly.

"Do you suppose we can make the hockey team?" said John.

James had a chest drawer open. "Look, Jay! They've even moved our clothes. Mother, may we stay up here tonight?"

"Look in the bathroom," she said.

Robes hung there and pajamas. It was complete.

"How did you do it? We never guessed a thing."

"While you were off mooning around the compound, wondering what to do next. The carpenter was making your new shelves the day you visited him. Dhayan helped make the spreads for the beds. If you noticed them at all, you probably thought they were curtains."

They did not discover the picture until they were alone. It hung above the bookcase, a tinted photograph it was, with a brook in the foreground, and beyond it a white house. Between, there was a tall willow tree. Home.

While they looked, a little lizard came clicking out from behind the picture frame. Its long tongue shot out and gathered in a chilled mosquito, attracted by the light.

"So that's how it's done!" John saluted the little creature. "I have to hand it to you."

The lizard helped the bad moment, and then James said, "Know something? I just got it. Mother means this room to be our Indian willow."

"Could be, Jay," said John. "Could be."

He sat down in the chair at the desk where his father had sat and stuck his feet out straight in front of him. He seemed to be studying his shoes, but when he looked up, there was such an odd expression on his face that James asked, "Now what?"

"I've just thought of something," he said wonderingly. "It sort of hit me, the way things do. We made a fuss among ourselves about leaving the willow tree. But we never had it all year round. We stayed in the house in the winter, remember?" He waved his hand to take in the comfort and beauty of the new room, their gift. "We can't have this all the year round, either. It's too hot up here in summer, except to sleep out on the roof, they say, until the rains begin. I've heard that somewhere round, since we came."

"Yes, but what are you getting at, Jay?"

"I think we were starting to be homesick before we ever left home. That's what all the fuss over leaving the tree was about."

James anchored himself on the other desk chair and faced his brother across the wide expanse of shining wood. "You don't say."

"I do say. I'm sure of it."

"D'you suppose Barby guesses that that's what has been the

matter with her all this time? She was plenty rude to Fitz in London."

"Well, it was his fault in a way that we had to leave home, but I'm not sorry now, are you?"

James shook his head. "No, and I shan't ever be, I'm sure of that. This is a good place, Jay."

After a while they went back to the drawing room to carry their gifts upstairs. "I say," said John, "between us we've got the start of an elephant collection."

He began setting them up on top of the new shelves, and a small ivory tusk fell out. "Here we go," he said. "Know where's some glue? They say these people never make anything quite perfect for fear the gods will be angry, because they are the only perfect ones."

James said, "Nice alibi. Maybe we can use it sometime."

He was unrolling the two friezes of Egyptian figures in appliqué that had Barby's card attached. She had evidently shopped in Port Said, too.

"Let's put these over our beds, the way we do pennants at home, only straight."

That called for thumbtacks in addition to the glue, and when they went downstairs in search, dinner was ready.

They had carols in the drawing room later, with the violin and the battered piano, ending with the Tennants' best loved one of ancient origin. It had been sung last on every Christmas Eve that any of the children could remember.

> *Infant holy,*
> *Infant lowly,*
> *For his bed a cattle stall;*
> *Oxen lowing,*
> *Little knowing*
> *Christ the Babe is Lord of all.*
> *Swift are winging,*

Angels singing,
Noels ringing,
Tidings bringing:
Christ the Babe is born for all.

A year ago they had sung it in the long living room at home,
with no thought of the change that was coming. Now they
were in India and already, after less than a month, the old land
had spoken to each, but with a different voice.

Barby was the only one who had refused to listen.

10: THE MISSING VIOLIN

Christmas came on Sunday that year, and Professor Tennant had been asked to do the morning sermon, even though it would have to be interpreted, sentence by sentence.

The church was as crowded as the Christmas program had been, and he was a little nervous, the family could see. It would be his first appearance before an Indian congregation. And he wasn't making it any easier for himself because he had chosen a very odd text for a Christmas talk.

He read it in English and the interpreter repeated it in Hindustani, phrase by phrase. "Unto him that is able to do exceeding abundantly above all that we ask or think, according to the power that worketh in us, unto him be the glory, world without end, amen!"

There was a little pause while people coughed and squirmed and a crying baby was taken out. Then he seized the lapels of his robe. The family sat back on the bench. Now he was all right. That lapel business was the outward sign.

"Christmas is a giving time," he said, "so that some of you are wondering why I chose to talk about prayer today. But if you read it again, you will see how closely it is tied to giving.

"Sometimes we ask for the chance to give something to others and it seems denied us. Perhaps we want to give the wrong thing in the wrong way, patronizingly, proudly, for show or business reasons. Real giving does not care for show. The wrapping around the gift does not matter if the gift itself is all right. Real giving does not expect credit. It is only when one's motive is right that the God-given power in each person gets its chance to operate in the best way. It is only then that the surprise comes, the abundance.

"Jesus was born as the gift of God to this world, and since His birth, two thousand years ago, people have been making gifts to each other in His name. Let us each answer a question quietly, you in the pews and I here in the pulpit. Have I asked as I should so that I may give as I ought?"

There was more, but he had already made a point his sons could grasp. They hadn't asked to go to this school, but they had liked the idea last night. Then it meant to them only their own enjoyment—hockey and to stay in this place that had become good. Certainly getting to stay here hadn't meant a chance to do anything for anyone.

Now the whole proposition took on a new meaning. If they got any good out of it, they'd have to put something into it. Last night their father had said if they made the hockey team, it must be because they were good players and not because they were his sons. That, too, was a little clearer.

They liked Dhayan Singh. But they had been a bit patronizing with him. That was another matter to be met honestly. They hadn't given him much.

Each turned and met the other's eye. This strange phenomenon of their twinship had happened before, having the same thought at the same time. It was happening now.

"Check!" John whispered.

From the Book of the Jays   December 26

We've had a swell Christmas. Even Barby said so. She likes our present. We had peacock that we shot ourselves. We took the salad, and THE LADIES, that's what Mrs. Roberts calls the ones that aren't married, brought the vegetables and the dessert. Mrs. Roberts did the soup, and her cook fixed the peacock. If you shut your eyes, it might as well be turkey. I did shut mine for a sec', but I thought about the way the fields looked and the blue line that was hills far away. I wonder if we will see any mountains closer to, while we are here? The girls will.

Our present was this room for ourselves that I am writing in. A place for all our things, and Mother says we can bring the boys up here. We are not going to the hills in March, but to this school, right now after vacation, that Father is acting manager of. Until Fitz comes. He is supposed to manage part of the time and to study part of the time.

Mr. Meredith, the police superintendent here and the owner of the gun Father shot with, was invited to the Christmas dinner. That made me lose a good stamp. But it wasn't his fault. He's a swell guy. He sat between Mother and Miss Stanton. He likes Indian music, but he wants to hear Mother play, too. He knows a lot about Indian instruments. He is coming to our house some night to have music. Mother invited him. She asked Miss Stanton, too. The stamp was because of an argument we had if there'd be a fourteenth person. There was, and it was Mr. Meredith. The Indians call him the *Kuptan Sahib*. John won, so he gets to keep it in his book for a while. I'll get it back.

James Tennant

That stamp had been their first major addition to either collection since coming to Rajahpur. They watched from the roof for the postman's appearance up the road and were usually on hand for the distribution.

On the second morning following Christmas, they sighted him early and came down to the front veranda to wait. It had rained in the night and there was a pleasant smell of cut grass and sun on flowers, mingled with the tang of wet earth. They could hear the faint tap of the typewriter from behind the closed study door.

A crested *hoopoo* swooped down with a flash of coppery

feathers and thrust its long bill into the green turf nearby, hunting a late breakfast. The high clear notes of the well song drifted across from Charity Abide.

"Nice, huh?" James offered.

"Only one thing missing," said John with a grin, "and that's a double chocolate malted."

And then their mother was in the door behind them, saying, "Come in a minute, boys. I need you."

She pointed to the piano. "Look! Only one violin. I discovered it when I came in here to see if I could imitate that weird tune they sing at the well. You haven't hidden the other for a joke?"

She looked at them anxiously, and they at her, wonderingly.

"You know we never touch them, Mother."

"I wish you wanted to. But if this is not a joke, then we need to work on it. I'll have to interrupt your father."

Dr. Tennant came out of the study, blinking a little, and heard the story. He insisted that the violin must be somewhere around. He was inclined to think it a fuss about nothing. "It's just been moved in the dusting. Have you looked?"

"No, not yet. I am really a bit frightened. The place is so quiet. I thought if someone had taken it, they might still be around."

"Which one is missing, dear?"

"I don't know. I'm afraid—wait, I'll open this one. You'd think I could tell the cases apart by this time."

When her shaking hands flung back the lid, red lining showed.

"Oh, oh, the best one's gone."

"Maybe not. Let's check."

Dr. Tennant strode to the door and shouted for Ram Gopal, who came on the double. He looked as anxious as they when they questioned him and shook his head. He hadn't seen anyone about. But he hadn't been in the room all morning, he reminded his mistress. That was because she had told the ayah to dust for him, while he set the storeroom in order. All those new boxes and trunks they had brought had to be put on bricks off the floor because of the white ants.

They made a quick search in wardrobes and bathrooms and on all the shelves and behind the long draperies, wherever anyone might have hidden the violin or still could be lurking. But there was no trace of a thief or of a violin case lined with worn purple satin. Nothing else, anywhere, seemed disturbed.

"It was silly of me to be frightened," said Mrs. Tennant. "And both violins are insured, but I wouldn't have minded so much if this one had been taken."

"Why is the other so much better, Mother?"

"It is worth more, for one thing, but I value it most because it was given to me by your—by an old lady, whom I still love very much. We had trouble and I—"

Her husband interrupted. "Eve, I think I ought to send word to Captain Meredith."

"Let's wait a bit. I don't want the servants upset or the children."

"But they are, already. It started the minute you asked Ram Gopal about the violin."

"If he is in the station, he'd be here inside ten minutes and I wouldn't know what to tell him. I can't remember when I last used it or anything. Wait a little while."

But waiting didn't help. None of the family could recall when they had last noticed the two cases lying together on the piano. Which one had she played Christmas Eve? She couldn't remember. Was the other one there then? No one could answer that.

By dinnertime that evening there was still no trace of the missing property, and nobody talked at table, except to be polite. The Jays went upstairs early. Working on their stamps might help them shake off some of the dreadful depressed feeling they had.

But the loss of the violin wasn't the sort of thing to forget that way, they found. So they went to bed and lay awake talking. The evening sounds of passing on the highway gradually stopped. A lonely coolie going home late sang a doleful tune in the quiet night. Somewhere a dog barked. Then the long roll of one night watchman's call to another across the city began its accustomed routine.

They heard their own man stumping around the house with his *lathi,* the heavy stick they all carried, and his lantern, and his muttered chant, *"Ram, Ram, Sita, Ram."* But his charm had not been effective, because the violin was gone and the thief not yet taken.

Whoever it was must have come in the daytime, when the winds have ears and one could have no secrets at all, so he must be someone known, with a right to come. But who of their new friends and neighbors would steal a violin?

Or perhaps a stranger had taken it and was still about, lurking, unable to get away, as their mother had feared. Each boy remembered at that point in their thinking that they had not searched the shadows of the roof top when they came up.

And then they heard the rhythm of the watchman's chant change to a growled order, followed by low talking. The thump of the stick sounded on the roof stairs, and the watchman stood at their door. Behind him, looking shrunken and miserable in the lantern light, was Dhayan Singh.

"One came," said the watchman, in vernacular. "And this is not the time of sewing, but for all to sleep. And there is no machine for the sewing up here. But he was ready to climb these stairs when I barred his way." He glared at Dhayan. "It did no good. He refused to leave until he had spoken."

The Jays were reaching for robes and slippers. John said,

"Very well, we will let him speak and he will tell us his business. You may go back to yours. This one who comes is our friend."

The watchman looked disappointed, but they waited until he had gone. Then they drew Dhayan into the room.

"What is the matter, friend? You look ill."

"I am," said Dhayan, nodding. "Here." He touched his heart. His teeth were chattering, though he was wrapped warmly in a blanket against the evening chill. He let it fall, and they saw he was clutching flat against him the lost violin. He had the case, at least.

"Dhayan! Where did you get that?"

"I borrowed it and now it is broken and your father will send me to jail."

He laid the case on the floor and folded his hands as suppliants do and stood there quietly, looking at them. His eyes were bright, and there was the odor of fever on his breath. The boys knew that. They had smelled it last when Mugsy had had the measles.

11: THE FATHER LOOK

The violin case seemed whole. Did the boy mean the violin inside was ruined? That would be the bad part.

The Jays locked glances, and their forefingers were raised in warning to each other that they should go cautiously.

John sat down on the floor and motioned James and Dhayan to sit with him. He made Dhayan wrap himself up again. He said, "You'd better tell us everything, Dhayan Singh. Then we will tell Father for you. He is manager now, so he will say what happens to you. But he does not send boys to jail. Besides, the *Kuptan Sahib* has become our friend. Mr. Meredith likes music too. Speak!"

"Ah, the music!" said Dhayan Singh. "Always I myself have wanted to make it. So much that the ache is here." He laid his hand on his heart again. "And the wish grows and fills me to own a *zithar* or a *sarangi*, something to make the sweet sounds. And then your family came. And I heard the Mem play. And I saw she had two things to make music with, though she only uses one at a time."

James said, "She needs two. Violins need rest the same as people do."

"They do? Two is better than one? Not just being rich?" The Indian boy's eyes opened wider. "That I did not know. Americans have so much." His tongue moistened his dry lips. "So, I made a plan. I would borrow one of those *zithars*, the American kind that belong to the Mem, and I would take it way off somewhere, so no one would hear and I would try to

113

play and then I would bring it back and no one would know. I did not mean to break it."

"But my mother locks the cases," said John. "How did you get it open?"

"Ah, that too I planned. With my fine small screwdriver that belongs to the sewing machine, I would take out the hinge, and like the walnut from its shell I would lift out that shining thing and I would play. I did my plan yesterday when you were all gone out at the tea at Miss Stanton's house. No one saw me, I think, because even Ram Gopal had gone with fresh starched *achhkan* to serve at the tea. I thought if anyone did see they would think I was coming to sew. I hid it in the bush, and after dark when the watchman was saying the charm of Sita on the other side of the house, I got it and went way off to the grandstand in the playing field. I made a little light where no one would see and thought for an hour I would play, and then I could bring it back."

"But one doesn't do it that way, Dhayan," said James, wanting to laugh at Dhayan's absurd idea. But the boy looked so pitiful. "Our mother has worked and studied years, more than we are old, to play as she does."

"Ah," said Dhayan Singh, "but because it was in my heart, I thought it would come. It does not come; that I found. Only ache and disappointment. The screwdriver slipped and the old wood in that case, it cracked. And when I lifted out that shining thing and the—what you play it with—ping, the string broke and curled up in a roll. And I could make nothing but a harsh, angry sound. I had wounded its spirit."

James got up then and brought a glass of water, which Dhayan Singh drank thirstily. He shivered and drew the blanket closer.

"There is only a little more," he said. "I was frightened when I saw that crack and when I tried to mend it with glue, a letter inside the silk got in the way. Letters are for sending. I know that. Not for tucking away in hidden places."

"I had to wait for the glue to dry to bring it back. And when I remembered those things the Sahib said in the sermon, my sin got bigger and bigger. I knew I could never make good music for any one until I had permission. I could not eat. And the wrong is burning like a fever in me and they will send me to jail."

He stopped and drank more water.

"We'll have to tell Father, of course," said John.

"Now? They must all have gone to bed by this time," said James.

"But Dhayan is really ill and he won't get any better until we do something."

"Do you suppose the violin is very much hurt?"

"Let's have a look."

Dhayan had tied the case together with a piece of hemp twine. When they loosened it, the broken part sagged, held together by the lining. The violin itself did not seem harmed when they lifted it out carefully and examined it under the lamp on the desk. The gut had snapped as he had said. That was replaceable. The case had received the most damage.

"What did he mean about a letter?"

"It must be here, somewhere."

It was. They found a square envelope, addressed in their mother's hand to a Miss Abigail Richmond, in care of a firm of lawyers in Bush Street, San Francisco. It was stamped and sealed but had never been mailed.

"This is odd," said James, turning it over and over, as though, if he searched hard enough, it would explain itself. "It's Mugsy's name, or part of it." He laid the letter on the table and began to tie up the case again.

John looked at the letter. "I think I'm going to have this

stamp, Jay," he said gloatingly. "Didn't you notice it?" He held it out. "It's that orange airmail we've been looking for. The six-center. Look at the funny old crate on it. Like a box."

"It can't be!"

Dhayan was allowed to sit in the blanket and shake while the albums were pulled out and John was justified. "There, older than we are. Older—I say, maybe the letter is kinda old, too. Wonder why it was never sent."

"We can ask," said James crisply.

They gathered up the violin and the letter and took Dhayan Singh with them down the stairs. They could hear the watchman muttering in the shadows when they slid the bolt of the dining-room door.

"Don't let him see the case," said James. "It will be all over the compound in the morning, if he does. This is some grapevine news we can do without."

Only one light was still burning.

"Father hasn't gone to bed yet, thank goodness," said John.

Dhayan was shivering again, and he crouched by the fireplace when they reached the drawing room. James switched on one lamp. There was no sound from the study, so their father had not yet heard them. Slippers were quiet on matting, and they had kept their voices low. James knocked on the study door.

John reached for the bellows to puff the gray ash in the fireplace into life again. He added a few shavings from the kindling basket and had a good flame by the time Dr. Tennant appeared. James had been explaining a little.

Dhayan Singh stood up. Dr. Tennant motioned him down again and pulled a hassock closer for himself. The Jays sat cross-legged on either side of the culprit.

This was to be the first of this kind of managing their father had done that they knew about, and they wondered what he would say. Maybe it would be easier all round that he was doing it now, and in this fashion. He looked more like a father than a stern school manager, in his crimson robe with a white scarf folded at the neck.

"He's sick, Father," said James, "and he didn't mean any harm."

"And there's the letter," said John.

"I understand," said Dr. Tennant, "some of it, anyway. Perhaps I'd better hear it all. Dhayan, you talk. This is your story. I'd rather hear it from you."

James brought a carafe of water from the dining room, and they gave Dhayan another drink. The fire needed attention again before he was through, but he had told everything, just as he had said it upstairs, though the voice was weaker now and it was plain his strength was low.

They showed their father the letter and the place in the case where it had been, and he looked at both carefully, but especially at the unmistakable handwriting that was his wife's.

"I think I should call your mother. Even if I have to wake her. She would prefer it. This boy needs some medicine and some sleep."

Dhayan stirred. "Not jail, Sahib? Not jail?"

"No, Dhayan Singh, definitely not jail, which is for punishment. Has not your conscience punished you already?"

"Already!" said Dhayan. "You speak true words, Sahib. Not many understand that truth. I only understood since Sunday. To ask properly that one may give properly. I cannot give music unless I know the true way to do it. There are no quick ways, only wise ways."

"And you are young to be learning that," said the school manager. He got up off the hassock and looked at his watch. "Midnight! Well, a few more words and then schoolboys should be in bed."

12: THE VALUE OF A VIOLIN

Dhayan sighed once into the folds of his blanket while they waited. Sweat beads came out on his forehead, but he did not drop the thick wrapping. The fresh sticks on the fire burned through and fell apart, and John leaned and emptied the kindling basket.

The lamp and the firelight made a little bright island on the hearth rug. The rest of the room was in shadow.

Outside the watchman stumped round the house again, stopping abruptly at the steps. He had seen the light. He pounded on the door, and John opened it a scant inch and said, "It's all right. That boy is ill and my father will give him some medicine."

"He probably thinks we are all half mad tonight," said James.

John did not answer. He was thinking about the letter. How had it got into the lining of the violin case when it had been meant for the post? Why hadn't someone—his mother—or anyone felt it there or noticed the bulge before now? His father hadn't taken the letter with him. Was it going to be a good thing that it was now found?

Mrs. Tennant came in alone. She had stopped to comb her hair, and she wore her best robe, a quilted one of a blue shade that made her eyes look almost purple. They seemed larger too, now, with her concern and question.

Dhayan got up and the blanket fell and the odor of his sweat and fever was strong in the room.

"You are ill, boy," she said. "My husband told me. And you have brought my violin back."

"And you are not angry, Mem Sahib? That is strange. There

119

is the letter, too. You will attend to it? It is meant for the post, to be sent, I think."

"More than you know, Dhayan. But it cannot go until morning, and you should go to bed, with some medicine to take. You need that more than anything right now. We will talk again when you are well. Here's my husband. You go along with him to the infirmary. The nurse will know better what to do for you than I."

Dr. Tennant had dressed again, and he carried his big flashlight. He said, "The Mem is right, Dhayan Singh. Come along."

When the door opened, a wave of cold air came in and the fire leaped up the chimney. Mrs. Tennant shivered and crouched down in front of it. She asked for the letter and John brought it from the table. She looked at the envelope a long time, while the boys waited.

"Poor Aunt Gail," she said softly. "I've been angry all these years because she never wrote to me after I sent her my apology and explanation. And she's been thinking me ungrateful and selfish."

"Who's she, Mother? Is she the one Mugsy's named for? Why did you have to apologize to her?"

She tapped her knee with the envelope. "I don't know where to begin. It's horrible to bring old hurts back to life by talking about them. Especially at this time of year."

"But you can't not tell," John protested. "Not now. We belong to you. We'd like to know if we've got an aunt somewhere. Is she really our aunt or just pretend? That much, anyway. Please, Mother."

His eyes met James's. They were going to be one ahead of Barby. She and Mugsy were still in their beds, undisturbed by the night's happenings.

"She's my aunt, Abigail Richmond, your great-aunt. She's the only living relative I have. She raised me after my parents were killed in an earthquake in Chile. Your grandfather was a mining engineer. I scarcely remember him."

"So that's who," said John. "Thank you, Mother."

She seemed not to notice John's interruption. She looked at the envelope again and sighed.

"I met your father at Berkeley. I was being prepared for a concert career. Aunt Gail had more ambition than was good for anybody to have. All my life she pushed me to work and practice and become a great artist. When I wanted to be married instead, it was such a disappointment to her that she wouldn't give up. She persisted, and after Barby was born she tried to bribe me."

"Bribe you! How, Mother? People don't bribe their own folks!" James reached out and laid a hand on her knee. "Don't cry, Mother. We're here."

"You wouldn't have been if I had given in to your aunt. She wanted me to leave your father. She said he'd never amount to anything. What kind of a life would I have as the wife of a poor professor. She offered to look after Barby, she and Martha, and I could go on and be a great violinist."

"So that's where Martha came in."

"Oh yes. Martha came to live with Aunt Gail when there was need of someone to look after me. She was nurse and housekeeper and companion, all rolled into one. She hired the servants and bossed everybody, went where she pleased, had a lot of friends."

Mrs. Tennant couldn't sit still any longer. She went to the piano, looking at the battered violin case for the first time, poking down into the lining and ripping it farther away from the wood.

"Why didn't Martha get Aunt Gail to see . . ." John began, and his mother interrupted, coming back to the fire.

"She didn't try. She beat me with words. She said if I left your father, I'd be the one who'd never amount to anything because I'd know always that I had betrayed my promises, my marriage vows."

"After I decided to stay with your father and he got the post in Jersey, Martha offered to come along and live with me always, as long as I needed her help, so that I could have all the time possible for music."

Her hands were limp in her lap, open palms on her knees as if she were pleading with them to understand and be kind. "So now you know what kind of mother you've got. Martha was right, and I've never been sorry I listened to her. We've had a wonderful life, this family, and don't ever let anyone pity you for being sons of a minister. I have only one regret. I wasn't woman enough to say good-by to Aunt Gail. I just walked out. This letter was my explanation that I felt I was doing the right thing. I asked for forgiveness, too, for all the hurt I had caused her. I was angry when she didn't answer and vowed I'd never willingly talk about her or my life with her again."

"How did the letter get in the violin case?"

"I probably put it in there to mail at the conservatory and forgot, because I didn't see it, that I hadn't posted it. Everything was in a flurry just then. It could have worked down through the pocket. I've always had a pocket in my violin cases for change and a door key if I should forget my purse."

They knew that. She had been the subject of many a family joke on account of it.

"Looking back, I can't see now why I felt the way I did about telling you. There was pride, of course. But I suppose I didn't want anything to spoil your growing up. We choose sides about things in life often without realizing what we are doing. I didn't want you ranged against her on my account, nor against me on hers. You see? Aunt Gail is very wealthy. She could do a lot for you some day."

"But she was wrong, Mother, to feel that way about Father," John insisted.

She laughed for the first time since Dhayan Singh had left. "There, you see. You are taking sides already."

They laughed too, and that helped her. "Now run along to bed," she commanded, smiling. "And let me tell Barby tomorrow, please, and Mugsy, as much as she needs to know."

The boys hesitated. Two things they had to find out now.

"What are you going to do about the letter, Mother?"

"Mail it, of course. Wouldn't you?"

"Yes, but . . ."

She looked at them, saw disappointment, and examined the envelope again.

"Oh, I see. The stamp. It's a good thing you thought of it. Six cents won't take it to America by air from here. I could put it in another letter and tell Aunt Gail that two huskies I know will have umpteen fits until that yellow stamp comes back. How's that?"

"Swell, Mother. Then she'll have to answer. But she'd better send back the whole cover. People do spoil stamps trying to take them off."

"We'll just have to hope that Aunt Gail's intelligence spreads to stamp collection. There, that's enough. Cut along to bed."

At the door they stopped again. "Mother, you aren't going to do anything to Dhayan Singh, are you? The violin isn't really hurt, is it?"

"No, I don't think so. It's only the case and the gut. I haven't the right to punish him, but I am obliged to help him learn some kind of music. Even your aunt would say so. I've been so busy settling this house that I haven't thought much about my part in this school. Maybe Dhayan Singh is showing me the way. Now then, good night. This is positively my last word, Jays."

They chuckled and made for the stairs. "Family mystery, family history, family doings in Rajahpur," James chanted on the way up. But they were solemn enough afterward in the roof room, talking it over a little before a second lights-out that night.

"I guess even grownups can make mistakes," said James.

"Martha must have liked Mother and Barby an awful lot— and Father, too, of course."

"She could have had it nice and easy at Aunt Gail's, I guess. And look what she's got with us. She's scandalized inside by these Indian ways. But she isn't griping," said James, yawning. "She's had a willow tree to miss, too," he added.

"Meaning what?"

"Oh, giving up things she likes and . . ."

"But she's seeing the world."

"And without joining the Navy, too." James chuckled.

13: EXPERIMENT IN EDUCATION

From the Book of the Jays   New Year's Day

Captain Meredith took all of us to see the New Year's Review in cantonments today at the parade ground. They had a march past and events like tent pegging and a horse going through a flaming hoop. It didn't hurt him. I asked Mr. Meredith. And band playing and trooping colors. There was an enormous crowd, all the ladies in colored dresses like a garden party.

We've got out of the habit of watching Mugsy on account of having the ayah for her, but this time the ayah couldn't go. Mother didn't mind, but Barby had a fit as usual when we saw Mugsy talking to an Indian man in the section of seats next to us. He had on a gorgeous uniform and a turban with gold thread in it. Where he sat was the private pavilion of Mura State. Mugsy said she could see better there, so she went over. It was only the Rajah himself that she was speaking to, and his second son the Prince Ranjit. When she told him her name, the Rajah had his secretary write it down and he said he'd invite her to see the polo some day. He plays and we've been dying to see it real close.

So then the secretary came over and took Father to be presented. The Rajah already knew Captain Meredith.

Mugsy's doing all right in spite of her name. Now that we know about Aunt Abigail, Mother doesn't mind changing it, but Mugsy does. So I guess she will have Mugsy on her calling cards and be an old maid. That's what Barby says.

John Tennant

From the Book of the Jays   January 2

John left out the best part. That was the white horse, carrying the drums for the band and without a rider. He had a black velvet saddlecloth with designs worked on it. But instead of a saddle, the straps for holding the drums were laid across. He lifted his feet high, as if he knew everybody was watching him. My, what a proud horse! Captain Meredith says there is a story about him. They say it is a very old horse, one of those the Emperor William gave to Queen Victoria. She was Colonel of that regiment; that's how they got the horse before they came out to India. It seems that horses of a regiment have their own papers, the same as the men. So, when it comes time every so often to retire those over age, that horse's papers get lost. Then they make out new papers with a younger age and it goes on carrying the drums. That's all it does, the whole year long, lead the parade on New Year's Day. Gosh! Imagine!

Two more days, then school for us.

James Tennant

There was nothing in that first day in the new school like any other first day the Jays had yet had in their school life to date.

Clothes made a distinct difference, to begin with. They had new khaki shirts, khaki shorts, and thick wool stockings that ended in a wide cuff just below their knees. Sleeveless pullover sweaters were for the early morning, to be tossed aside when the sun climbed. Bill Evans would hoot at such an outfit, the stockings particularly.

It had been fun, though, to go shopping with their mother in the cloth bazaar. And it was a little surprising to feel the friendliness of the merchant when she explained they were going to school with Indian boys.

"It will be good for them," he said. "And for all those others, too. Not one side nor the other has all the knowing." He measured the khaki-colored cotton gabardine for the shirts and the heavier twill for the shorts, with a long, slender iron rod grooved in inches and fractions.

"Jackets?" he suggested hopefully, before he tore the length.

Mrs. Tennant shook her head. "No, they have some tweed ones that will do nicely now. Later, perhaps."

The tailor's machine whirred every day for a week, getting the stuff sewed. The Jays managed to keep him in sight at least and to get a little closer occasionally, thinking they weren't being noticed. There was a trick with shorts they hoped he knew. Dhayan Singh was not yet well enough to sew. He couldn't help them at that point.

But if the tailor was patient, Barbara was not. "Mother," she complained, "will you look at the Jays? One on each side of the sewing machine. You'd think they were going to be presented at court, at the very least. At home, half the time, you get their things when they aren't around and they put them on and wear them. How'll I get mine done? Celia says I ought to have . . ."

A door closed on the advice Celia Roberts had given.

The Jays grinned at each other a little sheepishly. Who wouldn't want to watch clothes growing right under their eyes, sewed by a man, sitting on a porch on a cotton rug and turning the wheel with his hand? Bill Evans would think that was something.

Barbara missed a pet paint brush and a precious cake of brown paint from her water-color box. The ayah located them in the Jays' bathroom long after Barbara had left for the hills. The Jays weren't taking any chances that first day of school. The best protection was a duplicate of James's mole, under John's left ear. The sun had added to the tan begun in the Indian Ocean, which helped the make-up attempt wonderfully.

"Mother knows," said John on the way to school.

"She knows everything," said James. "What, particularly?"

"Duplicating your mole. I saw her look at us at breakfast."

"She won't tell. As long as she just looks, we're safe. It's Barby I'd worry about."

"Wait until she misses her brown paint," said John. "Come on, hurry; there's the bell."

The whole school gathered for prayers every morning at nine in the chapel. That was another new thing. There were no morning devotions at Chalmers School. There the Jays had a close schedule of breakfast, a stop for candy bars, three blocks from home in five minutes flat, a hesitation at their locker, and two seconds to get in their seats for history before Miss Williams got to the T's in the roll book. They usually made it but with no breath to spare.

In Rajahpur that first morning, sitting at the back and feeling awkward, they watched the new program begin to unfold.

The master in charge, wearing a long coat buttoned up to his chin sat in the pulpit with their father. At the right, in the transept the five other masters sat on the front bench of a section that was filled on Sunday with staff and employees of both schools.

The open-backed pews in the nave were filled with boys, who had returned in groups and singly, all the day before, from their village homes. The compound had echoed with the disputes of tonga and cart drivers and boys' greetings.

When the bell ceased, the boys stopped talking. A scripture reading and hymn were followed by a brief prayer. Then the master of the day made a few announcements. There would be hockey practice on the playing field after tea. New laundry squads and kitchen turns were posted on the bulletin board outside the office. The nurse would be in the dispensary at four o'clock. Anyone who had come back with a cold must report. They were to have two new day scholars in the school, the sons of the acting manager, Dr. Tennant, to whom he hoped all would offer welcome and help as needed. Would the two new boys please come up and be introduced?

The Jays had not expected that. As they started forward, they were conscious of the stiff new shorts scratching their legs. Their feet and hands felt oddly too large. Would they have to say anything?

They didn't. The master shook hands, presented them, the whole school clapped, and there was Dhayan Singh, looking a little pale, coming to show them their places where the sixth form sat in the left transept.

There were only six classes or forms, the Jays learned later, and the sixth was like eighth grade at home, except that the English or Cambridge curriculum was followed. They would study Indian and English history instead of American. Most of the work would be in vernacular. No one seemed to have thought of a way to get round that until Dhayan said, "You teach me the English better. I will read you the Hindustani and you will do the work from hearing, no?"

They were dismissed at lunchtime and then went back again until three-thirty. That would go on, the boys said, until the weather got too hot in late March.

"Then we have morning school and everything is over by noon. We sleep in the afternoon. It gets too hot to do anything else. You will see."

But for now it was cold until the sun warmed things. Then house and schoolroom doors came open and stayed that way until dark.

Government examinations for sixth form, a large class this year, would come in the middle of March. If they passed, some of the boys would go on to high school if there were scholarships for them.

That was another difference the Jays noticed. At home, everybody planned to go to high school and then to college, as a matter of course, a thing that was done. Here, if a boy was born to a poor family, he stayed poor unless an outside force propelled him higher. The mission school was that force for some.

Dhayan's great hunger for music and the way he had tried to satisfy it, an explanation and at the same time an excuse for that method, became daily more clear to the Jays. And because a proud woman in San Francisco had pushed her own ambitions too hard, an Indian boy round the other side of the world was going to have his heart's desire. But that could happen to only one boy in fifty or so.

Sixth form took the Jays in and gave them a place in their

life, as far as the boys could enter. A few weeks of school together would not give them a complete key to the Indian mind.
But it was enough for communication and more than enough
to make up to the boys for the things they were missing in the
United States because of the family's upheaval.

They kept their oneness and identity secret for just a week.
On a morning that they overslept, the mole painting was forgotten and a young master pounced.

"Ah," he said, grinning nastily and rubbing his hands as if
he had found something valuable. "I did not think Nature could
be so perfect. One of the Jays has lost his mole."

Sixth form shouted, seeing only the humor, but the Jays did
not join in. They knew that for some reason this particular
master did not like them. Their forefingers went up like a storm
warning, but the teacher did not notice. He called on John for
the first recitation, then James, in the hope of trapping them.

He would never do it, they were determined, though it meant
each must have a perfect lesson every day. Why had this master been so plainly glad to discover their little trick? It had gone
past a joke, they realized, and battle was now joined. They
would have to prove that they had not meant to cheat.

14: HEARTS FULL OF SONG

The roof room gradually became an informal meeting place for sixth form when games and dormitory duties were done. The Jays' education had been taken in hand heartily. They were learning a great deal that was not written either in English or Hindustani textbooks.

There was no place for them on the hockey team. That had been difficult to accept, though it was quite reasonable. They had figured it out for themselves. The boys now playing had been together for years. They had won their places by competition as well as ability. It was a new sport to the Jays, and they would only hinder until they could play well. There was a match with the Muslim Boys School to play off, and the second team at Government High School had offered a friendly post-season date before the weather became too warm. No, this was not a good time for the Jays to hope to break in.

It did not help that the sports supervisor was the master who had discovered their deception with the synthetic mole. He told them to report to his office one afternoon after he had noticed them in the crowd at the playing field, watching the two sixes in a practice match.

They had not asked for the explanation he gave them of their general unfitness for hockey, but they thanked him and were leaving the room when he called them back. They stood by the desk again quietly, waiting for him to speak. His lips were closed in a tight line below the narrow mustache he wore, and one of his hands lay clenched on the history notebooks collected from the class that morning. When he looked up again, they were startled by the glitter in his dark eyes.

"Why did you come to this school?"

James waited for John to answer, and John said nothing. What was there to say? And what right had this master to ask such a question? He had nothing to do with admissions. There was a peculiar tense feeling in the silence, and James couldn't let it go on.

He said, "We—well, we liked the boys and . . ."

"So you liked the boys!" the master repeated sarcastically. "What a reason to upset a whole school! Putting ideas into the boys' heads. Teaching them to want things above their station. Poking your noses in where you do not belong. You wanted to come here, it suited your family's plans, so it did not matter what might happen if you got what you wanted. It's a way foreigners have in India. We don't need you. That's the real reason why you won't get a place on my hockey team. I may have to tolerate you in my classroom, but on the playing field, no!"

"You might have waited until we asked to try out, Masterji." John's jaw was as squared as the master's.

"Silence!" The young man clenched his fist and struck the desk. "Now run sniveling to your father and get me dismissed."

"No fear," said John over his shoulder as they walked out.

"That's a thing we shan't tell anybody, mind," he said to James when they reached the silence of the roof room. They were alone because the rest of the boys would now be gathering at the school kitchen for their evening meal.

"But it's such nonsense," said James. "Somebody ought to know. We can't take a kicking lying down. *His* hockey team! My hat! I can't see that we have caused the kind of dissatisfaction he talked about."

"The fellow's probably got a peeve about something. But maybe it was a silly sort of idea for us to try to study here. It's

true that it did fit in with the family's wishes. Father and Mother wanted us here."

James said hotly, "Father and Mother aren't selfish people. That wasn't their whole reason. And I haven't noticed, not once, anyone or anything else being disturbed because we're here. The only thing is we'll do jolly well to get any kind of marks from him after this."

"Ah, we have him there," said John. "It's part of his gripe, I bet. The whole class is helping us. Look how fast we are learning this language. And the boys will know if we are good or not, so he daren't mark us down. Fair's fair."

James grinned. "Might be, Jay. Might be."

It was Dhayan who caught the master's wrath next day. No one but the Jays seemed to notice, and Dhayan himself said nothing. They hadn't seen much of him lately. Because his spare time was completely taken up now, he could not come to the roof room with the others.

The talk with the Mem Sahib had come about as she had promised, and Dhayan was making a slow beginning in music. Eve had looked at his long fingers and tested his ear and he had sung for her, one of the favorite Indian folk tunes for which there was no written score.

Dhayan's inner devils of doubt and discouragement were going farther and farther away as he sat each afternoon, when there was no tailoring, at the old piano in the house behind the pink vine and patiently worked at scales. It was Mrs. Tennant's idea that he should know a little of that, first, before beginning with anything stringed.

The family groaned. Wasn't Mugsy's tinkling enough? Barbara said, "I'm glad I shan't be here when he starts sawing on a fiddle." She stopped abruptly, horrified by a new thought. "You don't mean to let him use one of yours, Mother?"

"Why not?" Mrs. Tennant asked.

"What we need is a choir, or a boys' chorus or something," said Dr. Tennant, looking down the table at his wife, who was pouring coffee serenely.

"This congregation doesn't keep very good time, does it?" she remarked.

"Time!" her husband exclaimed. "What's that got to do with it? They could sing it dirge or jig if they'd only stay on the tune."

"And a chorus might."

"Might what?"

"Stay on the tune."

"Well, will you? Or won't you?"

Ram Gopal began passing the cups, and she had to look up

from the pouring. There was a twinkle in her eyes that didn't match her solemn face.

How much longer could she keep their father guessing? The children knew she didn't dare meet anyone's eye.

"She will laugh first, you'll see," said John, low, for only James to hear, he thought.

"Will I what? You mean stay on the tune? I always try to."

"Organize something, you witch, to get 'em on the tune and keep 'em there. The time will take care of itself." And then he winked at James and roared. He had made John lose his bet.

Mugsy said, "I knew it. She was going to, all the time."

"You knew more than I did, my child," said her father. "She hasn't said she would."

But it was like a snowball after that. Even the very little boys, who lived in their own separate dormitory with a master's wife to mother them, demanded to be allowed in the chorus. And when they were told it was only for the big boys, they howled.

"But we have to join," they argued. "The Mem Sahib gives them cookies and tea when they practice at her house."

The day that Dhayan Singh first drew a bow properly across the taut gut of the second-best violin, there were four boys on the veranda after school, waiting to see the Mem Sahib.

No one had given them permission to come. The housemaster knew nothing about it, and the school manager least of all. He was shut in his study doing an article about the ancient faith that had bred these schoolboys who were now Christian, an article that he hoped to see in print.

The callers wanted to learn to play something, too. If Dhayan Singh, whose father was a village farmer, could learn to make music of any kind, either of foreign or home inspiration, they could. It was not altogether a competitive thing, either, the Mem Sahib found out, after some questioning. They really wanted to. Evidently Dhayan Singh was not the only boy with a heart full of song. He was still the only one who had been willing to risk something.

The Jays were happily out of it. They had never wanted to touch either piano or violin, and after some discouraging attempts to keep them practicing, even Martha had given up. "You'll be sorry some day," she had warned them, but so far they hadn't been—not even now, in this sudden epidemic of ambition.

But they were drawn into it, after a fashion, when their mother came to the roof room for a talk with sixth form. She had written a note to Captain Meredith and had received an answer. After that, she had had a talk with the housemasters and their father in the study.

The gathering in the roof room was not a social one. There were no cookies and no tea. At the last minute Dr. Tennant came, taking the steps two at a time because he was late.

The boys sat on the beds and on the floor and the woman did most of the talking, at first. That was not Indian custom. The women let the men talk and they listened. The boys heard her out quietly at the beginning, and with cheers and some surprise at the end.

She said, "You know that I am the mother of two sons, though first of all I am my husband's wife. That is why I came to India."

The boys nodded at each other. That was understandable. It was done so here, too.

"Only third," the Mem was saying, "am I a musician, because that is my gift. All of us have a gift of one kind or another. It takes some people longer than others to find out their own. A short time after we came I knew that Dhayan Singh had found his, so I offered to help him. Then my husband felt we needed a chorus. Some of you are in that because you have good singing voices. But that is only helping a few of you. There are others who want to play and sing."

It was a long speech for Mrs. Tennant to make, and she cleared her throat nervously. James brought her some water.

"You will learn in time that music has the same principles in nearly every country, though notes are used in a different way. I find here a whole quarter note omitted from our western scale. You see, then, that you should be learning your country's instruments first. And I wondered how you could buy the expensive *tabla* and *zithar* and *sarangi* and who would teach you to play them."

The room was very still. Outside, the late afternoon noises came up to the roof, and it grew late, but no one stirred. There was excitement in the Mem's words, and they listened almost without breathing. She herself had to stop for breath, and then she went on again, up to her climax.

"It seems odd, sometimes, the way things happen and the happenings themselves are strange, unless one believes that there is a force in Nature which we call God, acting for our good, if we do not hinder. There is a man here in Rajahpur who knows a great deal about Indian music, and I met him and had a chance to talk to him about his hobby soon after we came. He is a man of whom you all speak with awe, and even with a little fear, I am afraid, because he stands for the Law. I mean the *Kuptan Sahib*, Mr. Meredith."

There was a little murmur then, around the room, and she waited until they quieted to finish her speech. "I talked to him again and then I spoke to your school manager and he will tell you the thing we want to do. I hope you will consider it."

That was when the cheers came, the moment they realized that this mother of sons was even yet only a looker-after-children, trying to do something for the boys who were in her husband's charge.

The school manager rose. "There isn't much more to say," he said, grinning at them, "except that I am not sure it can be done, though the Mem Sahib's plan is a good one. How would

you like to have a school orchestra with all Indian instruments?
If we can buy them, the *Kuptan Sahib* will come when he
can and help the boys learn to play. He is often away from the
station, but he thinks we have a wonderful idea. The money
is the big 'if.' The school has nothing in its budget for such a
project and boys never have any."

Everybody laughed and a few whistled.

One of the boys stood up and asked to speak, and he said,
"I think you mean we should start the fund?"

"There will have to be a fund, certainly," said Dr. Tennant,
"but it would be particularly nice if sixth form could start it,
something to leave behind you when you finish in May. You
are the oldest group, the top class."

At dinner Dr. Tennant said, "I suppose you know, Eve,
what you implied this afternoon? Not that the boys had the
faintest idea."

"What, among other things? That my husband gets the ideas
and puts me in to do the talking?"

"Neat, Mother," and "Well played," said the Jays.

Dr. Tennant looked as if his whole mind were on the selection
of a piece of chicken from the platter Ram Gopal held, and he
said absently, "No, oh no, not at all."

Ram Gopal said, "There, there it is, Sahib. The back piece
you are wanting, isn't it? I hid it from the *baba*."

Mugsy said, "So that's why I didn't get it. You just wait, Ram
Gopal."

The bearer pretended to be frightened and about to drop the
platter, making Mugsy laugh.

"He knows we men have to stick together, that's all, baby,"
said her father, and then to his wife, "No, my dear Eve, you
practically said in that part about strange happenings that because Mrs. Roberts decided peafowl would be the most economi-
cal Christmas dinner, we're about to have a school orchestra."

"Wrong again, Crystal Gazer," said Mrs. Tennant. "I go all

the way back to the source, as the man said when he claimed to be descended in a straight line from Adam. If Martha hadn't bossed me hard, once upon a time, we wouldn't be sitting here talking about a school orchestra."

"Eating chicken and having fun," said Mugsy. "I like it when you talk this way in different meanings from the words." Then she made a chime with her spoon on her water glass. "Take a bow, Martha; stand up!"

It was the first time since the finding of the letter that the matter had been referred to with the whole family present. What would Martha say?

She was very matter of fact. She said, "We'll wait and see if it's a good thing. When they get a treasurer for their fund, I'll give 'em five rupees for the honor. You can pick up the bones now, Mugsy dear. It's in the fashion and I forgot to tell you."

The Tennant family relaxed for dessert.

15: GOATS' MILK, LIMITED

There was no relaxing for sixth form. They had seventeen ideas about the orchestra, and the only resemblance one plan had to another was their need to raise the money for instruments.

"We could start a subscription paper," said one. "All the Americans on the compounds would help us."

"Everybody starts with them," another said scornfully. "Let's do this ourselves."

"We could sell something," said Dhayan Singh. "But I don't know what it would be."

"Have a concert and charge admission."

"You're starting at the wrong end. We have to get the *bajas* first and then learn to play them."

"If you want to make money selling something, it has to be what practically everybody will buy," said James slowly. "And that's food of some kind."

The boys looked discouraged. Everybody on the compound cooked their own food.

It was late January and they ought to be doing something. Instead, so far there had been only talk.

The Jays took the problem home with them to lunch one day. John said, "Martha, if you were going into business in this country, what would you sell?"

Martha was mixing chocolate milk. She poured it from one glass to another, considering the blend and the question. "I know what I wish somebody would do something about, and that's this blue extract from buffalos that they call milk."

"It says in a book at school that goats' milk is richer," said John.

"And how would we get that?" Martha asked.

How indeed? The Jays asked each other that question, shouted "Raise 'em!" and headed for school.

"It couldn't be something they ate," said Martha mildly.

"If it only were," said their mother. "Look at their plates. Scarcely touched."

"They'll live, though," said Barby witheringly. "They will flourish like the green bay tree, only there aren't any around here to prove if I'm right."

That was how GOATS' MILK, LTD. came into being. There was little accomplished in school that afternoon, and at three-thirty there were fifteen opinions, all thought up and ready to deliver. But the Jays had been thinking a little, too, and they were ready to answer all arguments, even those of the proud ones who objected to the menial work of keeping goats.

"There's good money in it," said John. "People will be glad to buy clean rich milk from us."

"But there has to be money in it from the beginning," said Dhayan Singh. "Money to buy the goats. Good ones, to milk, might cost as much as fifteen rupees, just for one."

"It's for the school. Why can't they lend it to us, to get started?"

"We could have a committee to find out," Dhayan said.

"How would we keep a goat?" John asked. No one had thought of ways. It was all means at the moment.

They couldn't organize a committee. Even the proud ones wanted to be on it. So they swarmed over to the manager's study in a mass of talk and waving arms. He received them on the side veranda, regarding them with his father look until they were quiet.

"Goats, eh?" he remarked, when he understood. "Sounds reasonable, but I don't know a thing about goats. I've never been in the dairy business in any form. But I know a lot about providing the working capital for private enterprises. This is more a public one, though, isn't it? At least the public will get the milk."

He sat down on the top step and took out his wallet, and the boys pressed close to see what would happen next.

"Now then, where do they get the best goats? Is this the season? Or should you wait until later to begin your new business?"

"Now, now, Sahib, please," said the boys. "In the cold season is best, when all the Mems are here to buy from us."

"How much do goats cost?"

Dhayan Singh said, "As much as fifteen rupees for a good nanny, Sahib, sir. We thought a good start would be three—you couldn't—could we borrow that much from the school budget? We could pay it back from the earnings. It is quite a lot of money, forty-five rupees."

"Yes, it is." The manager sounded thoughtful. "I don't think we should ask the school to start this corporation. You do have some money. Haven't the Jays told you about Miss Hammond's gift? She has given you five rupees, and I will give you another five. So we need thirty-five rupees. How much pocket money is there here in the crowd?"

That was a new idea. It took a moment to realize that they had any responsibility to the venture. Then they began to search pockets and knotted ends of shirt tails, and the Jays produced a small hoard meant to buy stamps for their collection. It came to one anna less than five rupees, a little pile of coins on the floor of the veranda.

Dr. Tennant gravely wrote down the name and contribution of each boy. Then he drew up an informal note of promise to pay and each of the boys signed, and he added three ten-rupee notes to the pile.

"I will put this paper in the school safe," he said, "and when you have earned enough to pay me back, we will tear it up and the goats will be entirely yours."

Mr. Roberts offered the car and his own services as general adviser on the buying trip to an outlying village. The Jays did not go.

"Let some of the others do this part," said their father. "You've given them a good push ahead."

The next day a farmer walked in driving the goats ahead of him. It was almost evening when he arrived. One, a black and white nanny, had two kids who were about ready to begin grazing. The two others were brown and black with long ears. One of them had a wicked gleam in her eye. They all said "baa" at intervals on the way through the compound, and they all smelled thoroughly goatish.

The boys had fenced in an enclosure underneath the

grandstand because Mr. Tennant had insisted on distance from all living quarters. He had also dwelt on a suitable place for taking care of the milk. It meant clearing out an old storeroom that had a stone floor. It meant more investment in the shape of buckets and pans, which no one had thought of, and a little charcoal stove to heat the milk on so it would keep, and straining cloths. Martha had a further hand in it before that part was arranged. Then the boys were on their own.

It was decided to make the venture an arithmetic project. That meant an account book for the boys to record the number of pounds of food bought, the amount of milk yield per animal, the amount of time the care of the goats and the milk took, and the income from the sale of the milk. They would know from those figures when they could begin to pay off their loan.

It would be a thorough course in simple cost-accounting, and the arithmetic master was delighted. He'd like all his classes to have projects, he said.

But that was before they found the black and white nanny dead in the enclosure about a week after the purchase. She lay on her side, bloated and stiff. They called a veterinary.

He said "poison" after one look and repeated it after the second. He had all the other animals removed from that vicinity, and another enclosure had to be arranged hastily.

The arithmetic master opened another page in the account book, slowly wrote "Profit and Loss" at the head of it, and underneath, "One nanny. Loss: total, after no yield."

The news reached the Jays on the way to school, which now led round by the playing field every morning for a look at the goats before chapel. They found all the others in sixth form by the enclosure and most of the rest of the school trying to see over their shoulders. A cart had come to take away the dead goat. The little kids were bleating so loud that everybody had to shout to be heard.

The warning bell rang.

"We can't leave them here all day," said James. "The vet says it isn't safe." He pushed his cork hat back and rubbed the red mark made by the tight sweat band.

"But where can we put them?"

"We'll take them to school, where we can watch them ourselves."

"How?"

It was a good question. The kids had no collars or halters, nothing but their long flapping ears to seize and hold them by. It was only a gamble that they would stay with the other nannies who could be tethered. So the Jays skipped chapel and went in search of rope and afterward staked the lot of them near their classroom door and no one but the history master was annoyed.

He gave his opinion freely. Who, before now, had heard of such goings-on, he sputtered? Indian boys playing *zithars* and herding goats instead of learning how to earn their living!

Sixth form moved uneasily in their seats and there were muttered answers, but the goats were not removed and the lesson began.

"I'd like to see him try anything," said James. "Then I certainly would go to Father. It's none of his business."

"Maybe that's the reason," said John. "Maybe he'd like to have a part in it."

"Can you imagine him helping us? He might get his hands dirty."

The new project was not an easy one. The routine prescribed by common sense to determine its business value took most of the boys' spare time, even when they worked in shifts. The sessions in the roof room ended, and the Jays were allowed to struggle alone with lessons. There was work to do now of a different sort.

It had helped to have the small boys make pets of the kids,

looking after them at milking time when they bleated loudest and feeding them bits of their own *roti,* the flat rounds of unleavened bread that the school cook made fresh for every meal. The kids grew sleek and fat, and the children forgot a little of their disappointment about the chorus.

In February the mission paper published Dr. Tennant's first article. Martha discovered it and brought the introductory note to the family at table.

"By Professor Philip Tennant," she read, "who is spending a year in India on leave from classes at an American seminary to study the ancient faiths of the east."

Dr. Tennant said, "That fellow Tennant has sold himself a bill of goods, if they only knew it. It takes all his time to keep up with modern distrust."

"What do you mean?" said Mrs. Tennant.

"Don't you read the papers, my dear? India is going to boil over one of these days. That Round Table Conference last spring didn't accomplish much. I keep hearing little pops and explosions all the time, right here in this compound. Some of these young masters are hotheads, if I ever saw any."

The Jays looked at each other. How much did their father actually know about the way one master felt? Did he know that they knew? They couldn't tell anything from their father's face, and John gave James a warning kick that meant "Keep still."

Martha said, "As long as they just talk, they'll work it off. It will be when they start doing something that government won't have it so easy. But we'll be safely home by that time, I guess."

The boys tried to find the paper afterward, to read the article. But it had disappeared. Much later they heard Martha telling their mother that she had sent it to Miss Richmond in San Francisco. "I guess that'll prove to her that your husband has amounted to something," she said.

In March Mrs. Roberts took Celia and Barby and Mugsy to the hills for the opening of the American school. Mugsy packed her doll's trunk again and went away cheerfully, except that she begged to take Sajida along.

The house seemed strange after the girls had gone. The Jays missed Mugsy's chatter at meals, and Barby's groanings were forgotten, a little.

"I do hope that Barby likes her new school," said Mrs. Tennant at dinner that first night. "Perhaps after all it would have been wiser if we had left her at home. But Celia has talked the place up well, and of course next year we'll all be going home."

"Don't worry, Eve. It will be good for her," said Dr. Tennant.

The weather grew warmer almost overnight, and the boys had a hard time keeping awake in school after lunch.

A new goat was found to take the place of the one that died, and sixth form stopped counting its losses. They had a customer for every drop of milk and were even talking of adding more to their small herd in July at the beginning of the new term of school.

"But we'll be the only ones around in July," said John one morning when it was their turn to feed. "These fellows will all be gone. Exams will be coming up pretty soon, and then school will be out, a real out, for some of these chaps."

"Tough, huh?" said James. "Then what about these goats?"

"There'll be a new sixth form. But how do we know any of the present fifth have got music in their soul?"

"Might do a little tabulating, eh, Jay?"

"Wouldn't hurt."

"Of course, we'll be here."

But what would they study? It was a new thought for the Jays, and a little sobering.

"Maybe we won't pass," said John. "They say these Middle School papers are something."

"It's a good thing our pass won't depend on these masters. We'd be licked by Mr. Grouch before we started," said James.

"Especially after that goat died."

"D'ya think any of the others suspect?"

"How could they when they don't know what we know?"

So the rest of the form went on thinking that there had been some poisonweed about. That must have been why the veterinarian and later the police inspector had insisted on putting the rest of the goats in a different place. All the grass where nanny had died had been rooted out. But no one except the police saw the small bottle cap that was found in it the day the place was scraped.

Government examinations for all Middle Schools were set for the second week of March. The Jays were to make the attempt, to see what they could do. The Circle Inspector had agreed to let them do the vernacular part orally. It was all highly irregular, he said, but these were changing times. And the school itself was in fine condition.

The goats were milked and the milk was tallied and weighed and sold during that grilling examination week but not by sixth form. The fifth had taken over without arrangement or plan. When it was ended, the Jays said, "I guess we needn't have worried."

Music in their soul? Maybe, maybe not. Businessmen anyway. They could count and make change and they knew how to milk.

It was the third week of March that the cable came from Aunt Gail. Mugsy would have liked it for its meanings different from the words. It read:

AND IF ONE PREVAIL AGAINST HER, TWO SHALL WITHSTAND HER, BUT A THREEFOLD CORD IS NOT QUICKLY BROKEN. LOVE.

GAIL RICHMOND

"What does she mean, Mother?" John asked soberly. "It sounds like poetry."

"It is poetry, John. From the Book of Ecclesiastes. Aunt Gail loves that book and so do I. She has changed the words a bit but it only makes her idea stronger, after all these years." Mrs. Tennant read the cable again.

"I think she means that Martha is the one who prevailed against her; that Martha and I together withstood her; but that she and Martha and I are a threefold cord, bound together for always."

"As you should be," said Professor Tennant. "Amen! I never thought to see *this* day. Stubborn old girl. Good old girl."

And then it was April. They began to have early school and everything was over at noon. The roof room became a Turkish bath in the daytime, so the Jays moved to Barbara's room downstairs. The overhead fan was set to a gentle whir after lunch and they slept, hard, as if they had done a long day's work and woke feeling dull and heavy.

The tea they had scorned on the boat now became a part of their Indian living, as matter of fact as breakfast food. It was a wonderful freshener, and there was indeed nothing like it, as the old deck steward had assured them.

They slept on the roof at night, out under the stars, each boy closed in to the narrow space of his bed by the sheer walls of the mosquito net, tucked tightly under the mattress. They lay awake, watching for the Southern Cross, first seen on the *Castalia*. It was like an old friend, come to recall other days. Life on that voyage seemed far away now.

It seemed to James that the changing seasons of India were almost a personal thing. They affected one's clothing, one's food, and even the way one lived. The activity of each hour of the day in the hot weather was governed by the degree of heat.

They were wearing their thinnest clothing now and envied the Indian boys their loose shirts worn with the tail out and the thin, draped *dhoti*, a length of cloth wound round first like a skirt, and then divided into trousers by pulling the end between the legs and tucking it into the waist.

The little white sweet melons from Lucknow began appearing in the fruit stalls in the bazaar, and Hyder Khan brought them home to chill in a large red clay bowl of water until breakfast time. The small bananas were gone. Now at lunch they ate long pale-green *kakri*, first cousin to cucumbers, which were cooling to one's blood the Indian boys said.

At night after the breathless heat and glare of the day there was ice cream for dinner, made with some of the rich milk from the boys' dairy. Two of the nannies were dry now, but the boys had also lost some of their customers when the women and little children from the whole station had gone off to the hills. The milk had to be used. The small boys at school were thriving and growing as fat as the little goats they tended so faithfully.

The account books, begun as an arithmetic project, were showing a good profit, and they had paid back their borrowings and now had two drums, a *dholak* and a *tabla*. The latter, played with the heel of the hand principally, had fascinated John when it first came. But it was too hot now to get excited about learning anything more. The last day of school was not far off.

Dawn was the nicest part of the day in that furnace-hot April. It was good to leave one's bed as soon as even a gray light appeared and walk about on the roof top in bare feet, opening one's arms wide to the cool air. Wood doves began their gentle kuckaroo, kuckaroo, off in some still dark, shady spot. Flocks of wild green parrots came awake, too, and flew shrilly away to feed. And always there were the crows, black against any morning sky, when they rose in clouds from their roosting tree with their raucous caw, caw, caw.

The boys rigged a shower in their bathroom with a pair of old square oil tins for the tank and a complicated arrangement of pulley and homemade head, holes pricked with an awl in a shaped shallow disk. It took a trip to the bazaar and a fair slice out of a month's allowance as well as a long Saturday morning on the roof with the tinsmith, but it was worth it, if they remembered to fill the tins every night so that the water would be cooled by morning.

From the Book of the Jays   April 20
There hasn't been time to write down the things that have been happening. We are keeping goats to sell the milk to buy things for a school orchestra to play on. One of the masters does not like us. We do not know why. Jay says it wouldn't be right to tell Father. It would, if we could prove he killed one of our goats. It was poisoned. That was mean.

Mugsy and Barby have gone away to school in the hills. In two more weeks ours will be out. Then Mother and Martha are going up to see the girls for a while. They will take them out of boarding school and all live together in a little hill house Father has rented for them. It is the custom for the mothers to do that. Nothing has been said about what we are to do. We are worried. Somebody has to look after the goats, of course. Father and Mother think children should not ask questions about plans. They will tell us at the right time. It is not always the right time for us, however.

It is hot here now. We sleep out on the roof. Dhayan Singh can play a short piece on Mother's violin, but he squeaks in spots. Everything is drying up in the flower gardens except the roses. It is too hot to write in this any more tonight.

                                                 James Tennant

Sixth form looked blank when the problem of summering the goats came up. No one had thought of that. "Ask your father," they said to the Jays.

"It may help us to find out about ourselves," said John hopefully. "Come on, let's try."

They tapped on the study door at home when school was over for that day and thought they heard their father's voice welcoming them. But when the door opened, they found the history master there with him. They started to back out, with a muttered, "Sorry, Father," but Dr. Tennant said, "Come in, boys. Masterji is leaving. He will not be back next term. You will want to say good-by. He has decided he does not want to work with foreigners any more."

They did not know what to say, though they knew their father was waiting for something.

Masterji spoke first and saved them the trouble. He turned to the boys.

"I suppose it is you I have to thank for this, for of course you have told. Spying on me and never asking me to your house, while a ragged village boy can come and go as one of you."

"He works here," John protested. "Besides, he has become our friend."

"And a master could not be, I suppose?"

There was no answer. He picked up some money lying on the desk, made a fierce, arrogant gesture of farewell, and went out, banging the door.

"What was it you were supposed to have told me?"

"Do we have to? He's really gone, hasn't he?"

"Yes, but I think you'd better tell anyway. He poisoned that goat. You know that?"

"We guessed, Father. He hated us and was mean to some of the others, the poorest ones, and most of all to Dhayan Singh. He said we made the boys want things above their station, things they shouldn't have. Why should he want to come to our house?"

"Pride, probably, expressed in the wrong way."

"He wouldn't have had anything to talk about, Father, not politely. He can't say anything but mean things. How did you know about the goat?"

"The police found the cap of a poison bottle when the enclosure was scraped. Careless of him. Though of course he denied ever having had such a bottle. He deserved worse than dismissal, but the police can't prove anything. The circumstances were bad enough. There was an empty bottle in the trash that could have come from his room."

"You mean he didn't really resign?"

"No indeed. I fired him. He's still surprised. He had no idea that I knew what he has been doing. I'd like to have got rid of him sooner, but we had no proof that he did poison the goat, though the police report showed that somebody had."

"The boys said the police came because of Public Health."

"There's more than one kind." Dr. Tennant chuckled. "He found this place wasn't a good climate for an agitator. That's what I fired him for. He was trying to get the other young masters to help him force some new rules on the school which would keep out boys like Dhayan Singh. It's ridiculous to even think about it. This school was started in the first place for boys who wouldn't get an education any other way. It's . . . it's . . . well, there's no use my fuming about it now. The chap's gone and good riddance."

"What will he do now, Father?"

"Oh, go and find himself an audience in the bazaar probably and have a grand time for himself running us all down, British included, until he says one thing too many. Then Meredith will gather him in as a seditious character. Now mind you, I'm sorry for the fellow. He's been snubbed terribly some time or other, and he's got politics and personal feelings all mixed up."

"He took it out plenty on us," said John.

"The real trouble is, there are others like him, and before they get their ideas sorted out, India is going to have some bad times. Some of these hotheads can't think straight. But this is over for you two, so forget it and tell me what else you've got on your mind. You came in here for something, didn't you?"

"We almost forgot. It's the goats, Father."

"Oh, those! Well, I can still bear a little more, if I don't have to smell them too. A very little more, mind, before lunch."

"Sixth form wants to know how we will manage in the summer when the boys are all away. What will we do with the milk? And are we supposed to look after them by ourselves when school is out? We'll be the only ones of sixth form left."

Their father wore his blandest look when he said, "Oh, but you fellows won't be here, either. You're going with me."

It was the first time anyone had said that they were going anywhere. By not looking at each other, they managed to seem a little bland and innocent themselves. It was worth the struggle to keep their faces straight to know they had smoked out some information when they hadn't been sure they could.

Dr. Tennant took out his wallet, and his hands moved too slowly, opening it and holding up four pieces of green cardboard that he laid in a row on his blotter. They were railroad tickets.

"For the Tennant boys' birthday," he said. "Even though it comes after holiday, their mother and I thought a good way to celebrate would be for them to do a walking trip with their father to the Kolahoi Glacier."

The bland faces broke into excitement and pleasure and then concern again.

"Father! Mountains! But we can't take the goats with us. What'll we do with 'em? And why have you got four tickets there?"

"Well the extra one is hardly for goats. I didn't give them a thought when I bought these. I think there are a few goats in Kashmir already, from all I'm told. But we could ask a guest. That's what I had in mind. Have you any candidates to offer?"

There was only one. They spoke "Dhayan Singh" together.

Their father nodded. "Yes, that was our idea, too. His father, in fact, has already given permission."

"Does Dhayan know? Is that place far? When do we start?"

"We'll need to study the map to answer about the distance. But Roberts is going along. We need him to show us the way, and he needs us because he wants the kind of trip we have planned."

"So now we have to settle about the goats," said James.

"So now we do. They can't take care of themselves."

Dr. Tennant sat down again and relaxed with his hands back of his head. He looked at his sons.

His father's posture reminded John of a September day in Jersey and James tilting back in his chair and looking up into the willow tree and saying he wouldn't care about anything if they'd only find another like it in India. They hadn't. But there had been a lot of other things. Who, and Bill Evans least of all, would have imagined their going into the goat business? And now they were going on a hill holiday.

Their father came back from his cloud of thought. "Got any money in the project fund?"

"Some."

"Then I'd say, get the gardener or the carpenter or somebody around the place to feed the goats for you during holiday time. Dry up the third nanny. There won't be any milk to fuss with, and the little herd should be all right. Fair?"

"Fair," said the Jays, "only we'll be selling goats instead of milk, at this rate, come September."

From the Book of the Jays   May 4

Tomorrow is the last day of school for this term. We won't know if we passed until we get back from our holiday. I will mind, of course, if we don't. But Father said he is satisfied. He said school is more than passing exams. He said our going to this school was an experiment, and he feels it has been successful. I guess I know what he means. I think having that mean master made me learn it. No one is better than anybody else. If they think they are, they aren't happy.

John Tennant

16: HILL HOLIDAY

The parts of the program on that last morning of school when term ended flowed together smoothly, like the halves of a slowly closing door meeting neatly and with the joining scarcely showing when it is finally shut.

The Jays sat in their place with sixth form, hearing the words said, listening to the music—the chorus doing a lovely arrangement of *Jubilate*—and the prize giving. Reports, music, prizes, benediction.

But James was more conscious of that closing door, the ending of everything. These boys had become his friends and John's. He was beginning to understand a little the way they thought; which wasn't much different from the way boys thought in New Jersey, U.S.A. When the program was ended, school for some of them would be completely over for the rest of their lives. That door would be closed with no place to put even a finger in the crack.

There weren't enough scholarships to go round, for one thing, even for those who wanted to study further. In several cases, he knew, there wasn't enough ability in the boy to warrant studying further. For a few others their fathers saw no need for more education. They had now learned enough to serve the family, enough arithmetic to buy supplies and not be cheated. Enough shrewdness not to let the village moneylender cheat them at harvest time, when they paid their interest. Enough history perhaps not to make the same mistakes others had made.

Enough? There was never enough of anything in India for

some people, not of the right things. There was too much poverty and disease, everywhere, the same as in some other parts of the world. James was beginning to understand that, too. A little. There were so few schools like this, and so many boys everywhere. They had seen them in the fields, from the train window. They worked in the bazaar and in other people's gardens. Boys no older than they, the Jays. And here in this place they were trying, with a few goats, to build the foundation of an orchestra that might satisfy the hunger of a few boys for something beside their daily bread. That wasn't enough, either. Not all of the boys wanted music.

He came out of his troubled daydream to hear Dhayan Singh's name being called. The headmaster was giving out the prizes and had come to the scholarships. There was one especial scholarship, new this year, donated by an unnamed person for the most worthy boy. He didn't have to be a smart boy or a good hockey player. But he must be the one who had the confidence of his class and his teachers and who was popular with the whole school. The staff had voted that this prize should go to Dhayan Singh. Would he please come forward? It entitled him to go to Government High School, Rajahpur, for one year.

Even the headmaster's upraised hand could not stop the low murmur of sound that spread over the chapel for a moment and then the spontaneous outburst of clapping.

Dhayan looked confused and half rose from his place between the Jays. Then he sat down again and said, "I can't take it."

But it seemed he could. A Tennant elbow on each side of him almost shut off his breath for a moment. Two vigorous Tennant knees gave him a tremendous shove upward to get him on his feet and on his way to claim the certificate.

The rest of the prizes, for sports and essays and highest standing in a class, were run through. Then the headmaster said he hoped they would all have a pleasant holiday. He raised his hand again for silence, got it after a pause, and the acting manager pronounced a benediction. It was a very short one. Then they were free.

Sixth form gathered in a huddle around Dhayan, curious about his scholarship. They read the certificate over and over, but there was nothing to show its source in a single word. It merely directed the recipient to present it in July at the office of the Registrar, Government High School, for endorsement of the fees and privileges it covered.

The Jays walked with him to the dormitory to get his bundle of clothes and bedding. He was still a little dazed.

"It should not be mine," he said. "I have not the right. A boy like me, to receive this! You should have let me say I couldn't take it. Me, who should have gone to jail but for the kind hearts of your father and mother."

"And their common sense," said John. "They know you will never do a trick like that again."

"And Father wouldn't invite a jail-somebody to go along with us on holiday," said James.

"And besides . . ." John began, then hesitated. "Shall we tell him the joke, Jay?"

"The sooner, the quicker, I say," said James. "Maybe he will then stop groveling."

"Well then, Dhayan Singh, your scholarship is given by Captain Meredith."

"No!" Dhayan stopped in the path. It took him a moment to see any joke in that. When he did, he said, "But does he know?"

"He knows," said John firmly. "And he laughed, too."

"Then I will keep it. If he thinks it is all right, it must be."

The boys paid a last visit to the goats. Someone had curried them well. Their coats shone and their small sharp hoofs had been oiled and polished. They were being turned over to the summer caretaker in good condition.

At home, the house had a bare look again because all the

draperies had been packed away with the cushions. Pictures were piled face down on the beds, and there was a row of empty vases on the mantel in the dining room.

Ram Gopal spread the boys' bedding rolls in Barby's room to be packed. Martha and their mother would leave before they did, going in a different direction, not even from the same station, and Ram Gopal was going with them. By dinnertime the place would be hot and dark and deserted, and they themselves on a train somewhere, roaring north to a Kashmir holiday.

They talked about it a little, drowsily, stretched out on the floor under the fan that afternoon, but it had no real meaning for either of the three.

Although it was his own country, Dhayan Singh had never seen the Himalayas. He had read in his geography, as had the others, about glaciers, but the *Kolahoi* meant nothing more to him than any other famous sheet of slow moving ice. It would only become reality when they had experienced it, were seeing it for themselves, at the top of the Lidar Valley, instead of looking at a picture in a book that someone else had taken.

Later, the Jays went upstairs for a last look round before strapping up their train kit. Anything they had missed could still be tucked in.

John went round checking door and window bolts. Monkeys and squirrels could make a fine mess of things, once inside.

"D'ya think we'll need this?"

James had picked up a coil of rope from the desk, part of their early goat equipment. The nannies had proper halters now, and strong leather hitching lines. There was a clean ring in the dust where the rope had lain. He made his initials in the middle, with his finger, tracing JT, a line below it and a figure two below the line. JT/2. John's was one. He had been born first. It was their laundry mark, and it had helped occasionally when the duplicate mole failed.

"We might need it," said John. "Better take it. We can stow it in one of the holdalls."

They traveled that night and all the next day until late afternoon, getting down at a bleak-looking frontier town that was the terminal of motor-lorry transport into the hills. They were too late for that day's long trip, so they booked a room in the station for the night before going out to look round a little.

The country had changed gradually on the way north, and after midday it grew wilder and more craggy. Cultivation had given way to rocks and fortresses. Now in this hot, dry place, the boys saw for the first time the hawk-eyed men of the border tribes in their full-sleeved, vested shirts and wide, flowing trousers. They stalked along arrogantly in the narrow streets, missing nothing, letting others make way for them.

By the next night the little party had reached Domel, a customs place, which was about halfway on their motor journey. They reached Srinagar, chief city of Kashmir, the following evening. They had come two hundred miles from the end of the railroad.

From the Book of the Jays   May 10

We are here and under a willow tree. It is on a bank of Dal Lake, and our houseboat is tied up there. The lake connects by a canal to the Jhelum River. There are seven bridges across it because it winds around the town. The name of our boat is Happy Days. All the boats have names.

We almost left this book behind. It was in Father's study because the light in the roof room would draw too many insects.

The cook on this boat is named Gulab. He wants to go with us when we camp higher up in the hills. This boat is good enough for me if Father had not made the camping plan.

People here have an awful lot of things to sell. They put

their shop in a boat and row around, looking for customers. I was reading a story this morning by the window in the lounge. Dhayan and John were up on the roof deck trying to rig a fish-line. Father says he will not eat a fish out of this water. He needn't worry. They haven't caught any yet. Anyway, the window screen was suddenly pushed back and all I could see was this hand coming through with a little gold-colored papier-mâché box in it. A guy was sitting out there in a rowboat saying, "I am bringing you very nice things, Mem Sahib."

I said, "I am not a woman," and he nearly dropped the box in the lake. I bought it, afterward, for Mugsy. She wrote a letter from her hill school and said she had decided to make a collection of little boxes because of her Christmas one to start it. All the children have a collection of one kind or another. This box has a blue kingfisher painted on it.

I like to watch those birds get their breakfast. They eat fish, so I guess that proves there are some. They poise, and then they dive, whoops, so fast your eyes can't follow. They come back and sit on your guy lines or the bow of the boat eating their catch. In two gulps, mostly. Their blue color looks so clean.

James Tennant

From the Book of the Jays   May 11

Father and Mr. Roberts are renting camp stuff for us, tents and cots and things and sleeping bags for when we go to the glacier. Father took Dhayan Singh to the bazaar today and got him some shoes like ours. Those are for him to climb in so he will not hurt his feet or be cold.

If this was all we'd have, living on this houseboat, it would be enough for me for a holiday. We see something new every day. And shops! Mother and the girls would go crazy. We went to Third Bridge today and ordered a tea table for mother. The man promised to have it ready when we come back from camp.

Gunstock walnut we asked for, the very best, with bamboo pattern carved on the edge and folding legs so it will pack flat to take home.

There are snow peaks all round the lake. We can see one range, the Pir Panjal, from our bedroom window.

John Tennant

They made camp for a month thirty miles away at *Pahlgam,* on a little plateau between two rushing mountain streams. The grass had been cropped short, and there was an odd, sharp fragrance in the air, mixed with the smell of pine trees and wet rocks and campfire smoke.

Dr. Tennant sniffed a bit when he heard the boys talking of it and made a search. "Wild thyme, I think," he said. He showed them a little plant he had pulled from the bank above the stream. "That it?"

When crushed in the hand, it gave off the same cool, spicy smell they had noticed in the trampled grass. It belonged with mountain water and sun.

They settled in comfortably in three tents, one for sleeping, one for working and eating, and the third for the servants and the cooking.

Dr. Tennant got at his neglected notes. Mr. Roberts wrote letters. The Jays learned to take baths with no better equipment than a washbasin and an oil tin full of hot water. They rode for the first time on quiet mountain ponies, used to the trails and steep climbing. But no one could get Dhayan Singh on a horse. He shook his head patiently when they argued. "I have my shoes," he said. "I will trust my own feet."

But he went fishing with them tirelessly, in quiet pools above the torrent.

They woke in the mountain mornings to its sound, dulled a little by the canvas walls between. They ate enormously of

Gulab's odd meals and kept busy at something all day, until their muscles grew hard and Dhayan's cheeks began to show a healthy pink glow beneath the olive skin.

At night the wind blew in the pine trees and blended with the roar of the water below, and Dhayan said more than once, "If the Mem were here, she would make it into a tune on her *zithar*."

A pilgrim route followed the stream at the back of the camp, and wandering holy men could be seen in the village when they went to the post office. Dr. Tennant talked to a few who could speak halting English. And afterward his typewriter, mounted on a leather-covered ponypack basket that held the kitchen equipment on the road, "rattled like crazy," John said, getting down the things they had told him. Another article began to grow and was later sent off to the American paper that had printed the first one.

Mr. Roberts was a good storyteller, they found, at night round the campfire, where they burned the piles of long rich pine cones the boys had gathered during the day. He told of ancient folk beliefs and weird legends about the gods and old romances in courts long forgotten. When the evening's tale was done, they could just barely get to bed, they were so sleepy.

Then a day came when the men decided that the boys were hardened enough for the walking tour to the glacier. At least, if they were going at all, they had better start. Mr. Roberts studied the sky and said he looked for an early beginning of the monsoon. There had been a few thunderheads about, but the hill coolies grinned at the idea. It was too early yet, they said, to be so cautious.

They had easily ten days before the need to break camp and start the trip back to Rajahpur. The tents were left securely guarded under the eye of the village policeman. Their sleeping bags and the rest of their gear, stowed in pack baskets, were loaded on a pair of ponies. And so, after an early lunch, on a bright dry day at the end of the second week of June, they set out with two coolies on the first march to the glacier.

The way led northwest through the pines, climbing gradually but steadily until they came out on the meadow campground at Aru, seven miles on, where they spent the night.

In places the trail was only a series of shallow steps cut into the face of the rocky cliff. Though there had been no recent rain, the stones were slippery with moss, growing thick even in spots where the sun got through. They were accustomed now to talking above the roar of the stream far below in the narrow gorge.

Once the path descended to its level and they crossed on foot stones. Looking back, Dhayan pointed to the crags behind them.

"Just one step, if he slipped, would send a man right down."

The coolies grinned. They had followed like cats, sure of their way. One of them, an experienced glacier guide, said, "But no one will fall. You have me."

The gorge opened out next day, and their march lay through thicker forest. They crossed the stream once again, making camp at a place where another smaller one joined theirs. One of the coolies pointed up the little valley and said, "Lake. Many fish."

But he could not persuade them to make that detour. They were not used to the altitude, even yet, and after the day's march there was an uncomfortable beat in their ears until they had rested. So only the coolies wanted to make the extra effort.

Far above them, toward the north, they had been seeing for several hours the snowy peaks in the region of *Kolahoi*. They were in sight of another trail end, what they had come these many miles to see.

The next day they saw the glacier, and it was nothing at all like any imagining. They had been climbing steadily and had been glad to come out of the forest and into a flat grassy valley.

But round the next bend of the stream the grass disappeared, and there were only boulders and the going became rough and hot. They had to pay even more attention to footing now as the path grew more difficult.

Around another bend, following the wild water, they saw what looked at first like a low-roofed cave opening, but out of it the foaming river was pouring with a great roar. The coolies gave a shout and turned to them, grinning.

"See, Sahibs, there it is!"

Even then the boys could not realize it. Later, when they had rested a little, the coolie led them inch by struggling inch up over the great rocks, house-high, at the side of the valley. And they came out on a level spot and straightened up to see a frozen blue-white expanse like a still sea, choking the valley and spreading back and up to the base of the mountain—*Kola-hoi* glacier. It was a quiet place. Even the noise of the stream foaming out of the cavern was muted here above the snout of the glacier. And looking farther up into the clear blue sky, they saw at last *Kolahoi* itself, hidden before by the ridge round which they had come.

They camped for a couple of days in a sheltered spot back a half mile, at the edge of the trees where fuel for their evening fire was to be had for picking it up, a different kind of pine cone here.

They saw the mountain in many moods, at sunrise when all the lesser peaks reflected again its rosy glow, and in the fierce glare of noon when the ice field looked more cruel than beautiful.

At night when the creeping shadows rounded off the sharpness, Kolahoi's spire became a shrine where the winds bowed before they drew up the cloud curtain.

Mr. Roberts was making pictures for slides, but he did not like the look of the clouds, and when the coolies agreed that it was time to go, they packed the pony baskets again and started back to their camp at *Pahlgam*.

It was on the last march, an hour or so out of their base camp, that the accident happened. Mr. Roberts's weather prophecy was coming true, and the boys were glad to put on their old jackets. The narrow path above the gorge of Kolahoi stream was more slippery with rain than it had been under moss. And it seemed steeper.

The men were ahead with the coolies and the ponies. The boys had slowed on that last hard push.

"I'm glad we didn't stop to fish," said James. "We had more time at the glacier, and we can fish tomorrow."

"Not if this rain keeps up," said John. "I'm for a nice warm, tidy tent, and some of Gulab's soup."

He reached for a low branch of a tree growing in the rocks on the gorge side to pull himself forward. Thunder rolled and a sharp crack of lightning made the three jump, and the little tree that John still held came loose in his hand. His feet slipped and he yelled, "Look out, there!" and tried to jump ahead to the next rocky step.

Dhayan saw and clutched him, and James watched them both go over the edge and out of sight.

17: ANIMAL HUSBANDRY

James shouted, "Jay! Dhayan! Are you hurt?"

He listened, straining to hear above the noise of the wind and the stream, but there was no answer.

Then he was struggling up the steep trail without heeding his own footing, calling, "Father! Wait! Come back!" He could scarcely talk when he reached the others. "Quick! My rope there on the near pony. It's John and Dhayan. Over!"

His panting and frantic gestures were better than words for the coolies, and none were needed when they saw the fresh break in the bank.

James insisted they let him go down because he was light. He was conscious of only one fear and that was what he would find at the bottom. He stepped off the edge and found himself going slowly down the face of the gorge, with the coolies paying out the rope, held stoutly by a firm-rooted pine tree. If only that had been the one John had grasped!

His feet touched gravel. He bumped a boulder. He was down. There was a fine spray in the air, partly from the rain beating on the rocks and partly from the wild current. His face was wet with it when he untied the rope from around his waist and started along the narrow bank to the spot where the boys might have lodged below the slide—if it hadn't covered them! Or they might have been dashed against the rocks. He dared not think of that.

These rocks and boulders were more difficult to walk on than those in the glacier valley, which had been dry, though much larger. Here his feet slipped on the slimy surfaces, back a step for every two forward. The hindrance was maddening and anxiety shortened his breath. Once he almost fell.

"Hold up, Jay," he muttered to himself. "If you are knocked out, what then?"

He stopped to rest and shouted, and went on and shouted again, and that time he thought he heard an answer. He found them round the next rock, Dhayan Singh sitting up against it and holding John in his arms, feet landward. John's eyes were closed, and he did not open them when James spoke his name.

Dhayan said, "You did come. I'm so tired." His voice was hoarse. He must have shouted a lot. His head sagged and his arms went limp, so that John started to slip toward the water and he made no move to save himself.

James had to think faster then, in fewer minutes, than he had ever done in his life before. There was John to pull up and Dhayan to revive so that he wouldn't fall farther. And with one pair of hands. He grasped John by his shirt collar with his right hand and John groaned when he touched his shoulder.

Both boys' clothes were muddy and torn. John's helmet lay at one side, a sodden ruin. A spot above Dhayan's right eye where blood was oozing was swollen the size of an egg. If only

they could talk! James despaired. What could he do by himself? But he had to do something.

He set his left knee against Dhayan's chest to keep him upright, and while still holding John away from the water, he
tried to get Dhayan's head back with his left hand and slap him
hard each time he did so. He set his teeth. "This hurts me
worse," he said. "Stout fellow!" But it didn't do any good, and
the blood began to trickle down from the cut again.

James stood a moment, holding John and panting while he
thought what to do next. If only the others would hurry up! He
tried to shift John so that he could lean against the rock, too,
and then the boys would give each other warmth. It was getting
colder and the light was going. It seemed a long time before he
got his brother, heavy and inert, pulled up against Dhayan,
with not a sound from either boy.

The slide had not been a bad one below the first fall that
John's misstep had started. The two were probably more hurt
from rolling down than from any weight upon them of stones
and earth.

James leaned to unbutton John's torn shirt and feel gently
for a heart beat. It was there. Better try to revive both boys. The
spray hadn't done it. If the helmet would hold water, he might
dash some in their faces. He picked it up and knelt carefully,
holding it against the rushing current.

And then he heard a shout and saw the grinning glacier
coolie coming round the bend in the stream. He had gone all
the way back to the place where the path descended to it and
had clambered along from rock to rock forward, as James had
done from the opposite direction.

James dropped the helmet. He wanted to shout and sing, but
his throat tightened instead and he couldn't say a word. The
coolie was coming fast, getting over the rocks better than he had
done. Maybe he would have a good idea what to do for the
boys.

And cheers, there was the other chap, following. But he was not grinning. His mournful face didn't change when he saw the boys. He shook his head and went to work on Dhayan, seeing the first man bent over John.

They used their hands to splash water over the unconscious faces, and after a while the boys did speak, mumbling a little about what had happened. It took longer to get them on their feet.

John said, "Help Dhayan. He . . . saved . . . me. My face . . . in the water. He . . . help me stand up. Ouch! My arm . . . don't touch."

Both the boys were bruised and stiff, but they insisted on walking, and the going was slow back to the path.

The men were there with the ponies. After the first anxious questioning John's father used his energy in action. He dug round in a pack basket and pulled out a shirt to rig a sling for John's sagging shoulder. All the kit was unslung so that John and Dhayan could ride. The big electric torch made a warm circle of light to work by. Because of it they could go on and not have to camp by the stream for the night.

The others carried the extra gear on their backs and guided the ponies up the steep path again, with the flashlight marking trail every foot of the way. It was slow going and very late when they reached the dark tents under the pines.

Even there not much more could be done for the boys' hurts. No doctor on the mountain, no car to drive them down at this hour of night to Srinagar City. Everything had to wait until morning.

They left in two parties next day, Mr. Tennant and John and Dhayan, early, while Mr. Roberts stayed with James and Gulab to pack up. They paid off the coolies at the lorry station, with extra *baksheesh* for the two who had gone to the glacier with them.

Back in the houseboat, Gulab hailed his crew aboard, and

they poled Happy Days nearer to the top of the lake, where James and his father would have a shorter walk to visit the boys while they were in the Cottage Hospital. John's collarbone was broken and both had been given treatment for shock.

They were delayed a week, and school had begun again by the time they were able to return to Rajahpur. John wore a big sling to rest his cast in and Dhayan still had a plaster over his eye.

The monsoon had set in on the plains, but it wasn't raining when their train stopped. There had been a downfall in the night leaving pools along the road, reflecting the tonga in the water as they went by. Everywhere hedges were green again and flowers were blooming once more in the gardens that had been so bare and dry when they went away.

The Jays hadn't expected to see their mother, but when the tonga stopped under the porte-cochere, she was standing in the doorway.

"I thought I heard wheels," she said.

She touched John's sling with her finger, making no fuss. She shook hands with Dhayan Singh, which embarrassed him. "They've written me what you did," she said. "Thank you is all I can say now, but we will never forget our debt to you."

She had a meal for them already laid in the dining room, and afterward, when John had gone with his father to see the station doctor, Dhayan and James climbed to the roof room to put some of the hill gear away. There, in the dust, still faintly visible, was the laundry mark James had so carelessly rubbed in with his finger. "We will still need this, thanks to you, stout fellow," he said, and grinned.

It was warm in the roof room, but the sickening heat of the end of school had gone. This was a moist heat, somewhat like sitting in a Turkish bath most of the time.

"It rains a lot for a few days," said Dhayan. "Then it clears and we put our beds out in the sun. Then it rains some more, maybe for a long time, and mold collects on shoes and insects eat your clothes. And there is nothing you can do about it. But it's my country. It's like this every year." He shrugged his shoulders and they both laughed at the doleful picture he had made.

"And it stops altogether, sometimes early, sometimes late, after sometimes a good rainfall and sometimes a bad one. If it has been poor, prices go up because the grain crop will be less. Good or bad we begin hockey again and have fun. That is the monsoon. But this isn't a bad country, nay?" He looked at James, hopeful of approval.

"Dhayan, you clown! It's a wonderful country. It has everything."

"But you are going away when the cold weather comes."

"Families have to go where the father does. Ours has to go back to his work."

"Why may this not be his work? He's been a good Sahib to us. He knows boys."

"He had us to practice on before we came here, remember?"

"Yes, you with your private enterprises. I knew what he meant the day we asked for the goat money."

"The goats! How could we forget them? Let's go."

They clattered down the stairs again and were off up the road to the goat pen. There were two new kids, which a brown and black nanny had produced that morning. She was the one with the look in her eye. Her son, staggering around butting his nose against the boards, had the look too, and he was coal black, not a hair off color. Before he was an hour older, he had a name, Shaitan, meaning devil.

The examination results were in the mail, waiting on Dr. Tennant's desk. The experiment had not been successful from one angle. The Jays had not passed. The language handicap had been too much.

Today was our birthday. We had good presents. That was just the parents' guff, to let us think the trip would be our only present. Mother invited Dhayan to dinner. She likes her tea table that we got in Kashmir very much.

They call us *gadariya* now, which means goatherd in Hindustani. It is because of our project. Father had planned some trips for us after holiday, the kind that teach you as much as lessons. But that was out when Jay got hurt. He can't do much of anything for a while, now. Dr. Jamna Das said it was a very bad break, and if he should have another accident before it gets well, he might not be able to use that arm very well the rest of his life. So we will stay put for a while.

At home if anybody fails in a class, they take it over. If we weren't going home in a few months, we would here.

Jay had to go for X rays of his bone, and he told Dr. Das about the goats. Then comes a letter to Father, about a sort of regular contract to furnish milk for the hospital.

Another nanny has kids now. We planned to sell them. But Father and the math master talked, and they asked us how we would like to start a real herd. Father called it animal husbandry. He said if it was in books to learn, we could, so he ordered a book about goats from Bombay. We've already got Shaitan for breed when he gets big enough. The whole school would have roared anyway if we had tried to sell him. Sure a spoiled billygoat, that one.

The hardest part was dairy sheds. Real ones. We had a meeting and the master reported our money. We are buying a couple of *banslis,* that's Indian flutes, for the orchestra, and using the rest of the cash for lumber. Father pretends to hold his nose when I come in from there before I have my bath. The carpenter and I have done most of the work. It's fun.

Father says the goats may run the school out of business. But he just jokes. It will be a new trade for some of the boys to learn. Not all have music in their soul. The goat book came last week. It was Jay's turn for a stamp. That was good because he can work at them with one hand, while I drive nails.

After school there is always a crowd of lower school, watching. Father says we are a good example, as a PK (Preacher's Kid) should be. We thought we wouldn't have to be one out here. But it follows you. The idea is that because of this caste business, they think working with your hands is beneath one. It does save blisters, maybe, to be a high caste. But I'm glad we haven't got it in America.

James Tennant

From the Book of the Jays   September 10
   I am too busy being a goatherd to write in this.
James Tennant

From the Book of the Jays   October 15
   Jay's bone is all right. He is out of his sling. The sheds are finished and my blisters are peeling. Dhayan comes over weekends for his violin lesson. He does not like his new school as well as this one.
James Tennant

And then it was November and the Tennants' year in India was almost over. In a little while, at the annual meeting of the mission, Philip Tennant would be free to take his research notes, his experiences, and his family back to America. In a little while now they would all be on the ocean once more, returning to the white house with a willow tree in its back yard.

The children would take the Willow House chairs out of the basement. They might even mend the broken leg of the rickety table and give a coat of fresh paint to the old cupboard. But nothing would be the same there, not ever again. How could it be?

The Jays talked it over, up in the roof room. "Mother knew what she was saying," said John. "Being with people you like, in a good place, counts most." He waved his hand, taking in the room, the roof, the compound, the school. "This is a good place, and we've never had a friend like Dhayan Singh."

"You mean then that you don't want to go home?" James asked.

"Do you?"

James grinned. "We are funny folks," he said. "We didn't think we wanted to come out here. But a family goes with the father unless he's an engineer and has to go where it is hard for a family to get to, like Upper Canada, or Thibet, or . . . or . . . well, places like that. We've had a wonderful time here when we thought we mightn't. Except your bone, of course. Maybe we will like it when we get home. I will like showing Bill Evans our stamps. I bet we've got some he hasn't."

"Stamps!" said John with disgust. "He can read about those in any stamp book. Dhayan won't be there. And we haven't seen half of the places here we want to see. South India, for one."

James said, "I was just testing. So you don't want to go home? I don't either. But there isn't anything we can do about it."

"We could ask the bishop," John urged. "It's Rajahpur's turn to have the annual meeting. I heard Mother and Mrs. Roberts counting up how many eggs for fifty people for breakfasts. The bishop will be here to have some of those eggs next week."

"But what if Father doesn't want to stay?" James looked troubled.

"He doesn't want to go. You watch him when he thinks nobody is looking. He didn't eat his oatmeal this morning."

"You can just not like oatmeal seven times a week without being sorry to go away from a place," James argued.

John wouldn't give up. "It's the way Martha and Mother lift their eyebrows and cock 'em at his plate and then nod at each other. Somebody ought to do something."

"But we haven't got anything to say about it. The children go where the father goes. That's why we had to come along in the first place. Remember?" said James.

"But suppose he wants to stay, no matter what we want, and they don't know it, the mission people, I mean? Shouldn't we tell? Maybe they'd be glad to know."

James was practical. "What kind of work would Father do if they did ask him to stay? Fitz will be coming for the school. That was the way it was planned. They won't just make a job for him because he likes India and is learning a lot and his children have made friends and the cook now likes Martha. Be reasonable, Jay."

"I can be," said John, grinning. "One night in camp when we were supposed to be asleep, the men were talking around the fire and Mr. Roberts said they'd like to take leave this year and go home with Celia instead of just sending her with someone. She's going this year, you know that?"

"And how I know it. How could anyone help but know it? Going home is all Barby talks about in her letters lately. She can't wait. All the things she and Celia will do on the boat and after they get home. You'd think Celia was a more special friend than anyone at home."

"She is, in a way," said John. "We four used to sit under that tree and shut the whole world out. D'ya think that was so good, huh, Jay?"

"Maybe it wasn't," said James slowly. "Maybe that's why we don't want to rush right back to it this fall. H'm. I hadn't thought of that."

"It can wait," said John. "We've got to concentrate on this other thing. Getting Father another job. Let's go and see the bishop when he comes. I can't see how it would hurt, and it might help."

James thought it over and decided it wouldn't hurt, just to talk to the bishop. He was a jolly, fat American who lived in Lucknow when he wasn't visiting annual meetings and laying cornerstones and starting new churches.

Then time leaped for everyone. The girls came back from the hills. The third nanny produced her seasonal kids. The hockey field was alive with boys every afternoon after school.

Overnight it was December tenth and people were expected to arrive the next day for the annual meeting. Every spare room in all the mission houses was ready, with extra beds placed on enclosed porches. The little house waiting for Fitz was achingly clean, converted into a dormitory for the LADIES, with beds set out in rows even in the living room for the week's duration.

The Tennants were having lunch that day, and after the fruit was served, Mrs. Tennant leaned back in her chair and said comfortably, "Everything is ready, down to the last spoon. There can't be a hitch anywhere. We've worked so hard that it ought to be a wonderful gathering. Too bad it will be only this one time for us."

The Jays' eyes met and two forefingers went up briefly. One more reason why it would be a good idea for them to go to the bishop. Mother wouldn't mind staying, either. They looked cautiously at their father. He was frowning at his plate and didn't seem to have heard a word that was said.

It was then they heard tonga bells jingling closer and closer and the voice of the driver when it halted and the thump of luggage being dropped on the veranda. The tailor was there, sewing a new dress for Barby, and he and the driver exchanged greetings. But there was no other voice to indicate who had come.

Mrs. Tennant stood up, ready to go and greet the guest, whoever it might be, but before she could take a step, there was a crash of chords from the piano and a fine baritone was singing to his own accompaniment, "Hail, hail, the gang's all here."

Fitz was announcing himself.

The family flowed out behind Mrs. Tennant to greet him, all but Barbara who sat on at the table, staring at her plate.

18: THE BISHOP SMILED

Fitz looked completely at home in India already. He was dressed in khaki shorts and shirt and wore knee-top ribbed socks of the same sort the Jays wore. He'd been carrying a swagger stick, too. The boys spied it at once, lying on top of his beaten-up bedding roll. Captain Meredith carried one most of the time.

"How come you are arriving this time of day?" Dr. Tennant demanded. "There's no mail train due in here until . . ."

"Oh, that," said Fitz airily. "Had my cable arrived, 'twould be no mystery. I've been touring a bit. I went from Bombay to Agra and then to Delhi. The bedroll is a borrow from a chap in England."

"And this?" John asked, twirling the swagger stick like a drum major's baton.

"Good for fending off beggars and pi dogs in the bazaar when you're touristing," said Fitz. He looked at Mrs. Tennant hopefully. "A tune, maybe, ma'am? A small one?"

She shook her head and shooed him away with the boys upstairs. "You'll have to sleep under the stars for a bit, Fitz, until the meeting is over and you can get into your own house."

"A house all to myself!" he exclaimed. "It's downright unsociable and a sin and waste of good space. I should be having my own lady to keep me company."

"Of course," said Mugsy, clapping her hands, "the very thing. And I'll be the bridesmaid. When is she coming so we can have a wedding?"

"Not for a year, nor a day," said Fitz. "Give her time, child, give her time. Come here."

He leaned down and whispered, but loud enough for all to hear what he said. "I haven't asked her yet."

He winked at the others, and then he sighed and shook his head and docilely followed the boys through the empty dining room and up the stairway.

When he had unpacked and put away the many astonishing things he turned out of his bed roll, they drew him to the parapet and pointed out the landmarks of the whole small estate.

The roof top was a pleasant, drowsy place at early afternoon during this season. From far across the yards they could hear the well-song sung melodiously by the gardeners at Charity Abide while the white bullocks plodded up the ramp and down again, drawing water for onions and roses to grow.

Children's voices echoed happily up to the roof top, too. They could be seen playing a mad game behind the motor sheds, where the father of five of them was mending a tire.

There were pleasant smells on the wind, too, roses and cork tree blossoms with the soapy smell underneath of the dishwater just thrown out behind the cookhouse.

So Fitz was introduced to part of his new life. "The place is almost self-contained," he remarked, "like a busy little anthill. So I'll be an ant if I can't be a husband for a while."

"You mustn't mind Mugsy," said John. "She's a bit cheeky, but only when she likes a person."

"So then one doesn't mind it at all. But your sister Barbara, now. I wish . . . one wishes . . . she might ever be a little bit cheeky. She keeps herself to herself a bit over much, wouldn't you say?"

What could anyone say? The Jays' eyes questioned each other miserably, and Fitz saw.

"I say, have I done something she doesn't like? Out with it, you young rascals, or I'll . . . I'll . . . I noticed she wasn't on the welcoming committee just now. Here, though, h'm?"

"Well you see, Barbara didn't want us to come out to India and she thought . . ."

John looked at James and James took over. "She felt you had studied enough—it wasn't just you, she would have felt that way about anybody—and if you hadn't insisted on going to school another year, we needn't have come."

Their confession couldn't have been so terrible, after all, because Fitz laughed hard. Then he sobered and said, "The poor little girl, what a lot I've got to make up to her, if she'll only let me."

He looked at his watch then and plunged into his bath, reminding them that their mother had said tea would be laid at exactly four. "We've been up here gossiping all the afternoon and that's mostly what women do."

He admired their shower system, and in between gasps he shouted at them through the curtain.

"It isn't what Barbara thinks, entirely," he spluttered. "They could have got somebody besides your father, but I asked for him. I'd heard of his work. And, the seminary liked the idea because they felt your father's work would benefit and then the school would be helped by this year of research and such. You see?" He emerged rubbing his wet hair and whooshing like a porpoise. "Ah, I'll have another contraption like this in my house."

Fitz was circumspect at tea and formal with Barbara, who only looked more angry when she had no chance to snub him again.

The bishop arrived that midnight from Lucknow and was given a room at the Robertses', which he turned into an office in no time, and announced that anyone who had private business with him would find him there.

And so the Jays did, having stalked him successfully all the way from the mess tent after lunch on the second day of the meeting.

"So you have come to help me, too, have you," he said, laughing, when they got round to their business. "Your sisters were here this morning."

They waited while he polished his glasses. They didn't look at each other but separately wondered what Barby and Mugsy had said to this big, pleasant man? Were they going to spoil everything? Mugsy wouldn't certainly, if she knew what she was doing, but they weren't certain about Barbara.

"Well, boys, you leave this to me, and don't you worry. I'll do my best for all. Every case is a little different. For instance, what will they do in America if I send a cable and say"—he reached for a pad and began to write as he talked—"something like this—IMPERATIVE TENNANT REMAIN INDIA URGE EXTENDED LEAVE FROM SEMINARY. H'm? What do you think they would do?"

"They'd find somebody," said John stoutly.

Barby and Mugsy didn't say a word about going to see the bishop, so the Jays didn't. It was an anxious week. The boys

didn't enjoy it as much as they had thought they would, seeing
so many Americans together, because they were constantly on
the watch for any chance word or crumb of intelligence that
might guide them as to what was going on. Their only consola-
tion was that a man who could smile the way the bishop did
couldn't do anything very awful about people's jobs.

But they didn't find out a thing, and the last morning of the
meeting came, the time when the bishop read out everybody's
assignment for another year. Their pulses were jumping when
the big man rose to read from the paper in his hand. Rajahpur
would come last because they were the host station this year.

They heard the names of places they didn't know were on
the map, and there seemed to be a great many of them before
the bishop came to Rajahpur. At that point he took off his
glasses and tapped his paper with them.

"Even an old bishop can have new experiences," he said. "I
have had one, here, this week."

The grownups looked at each other, and eyebrows worked
up and down in quiet questioning. Philip Tennant and his
wife, sitting together on the front seat with all their children,
looked straight ahead.

"A man's boys and girls were afraid he was going to make a
mistake because of them. If he were to return to America now,
they said, he would be leaving, in a way, an unfinished job.
They like us and want to stay, too, but they didn't emphasize
that. It was their father's work they were pleading for. So I sent
a cable and received the answer this morning."

He pulled a yellow slip from his pocket and read it aloud:

"RELEASE TENNANT REGRETFULLY FOR RAJAHPUR."

Everybody clapped so hard he couldn't go on for a moment,
but when he lifted his hand and they stopped, he said, "I'm
going to do a new thing this morning, beginning a new custom.
We believe in the family in India. It is the unit on which everything is built. But when we appoint a man to a station, we

sometimes forget his family, though they have to go along with him. So, today I am going to appoint a whole family to a place with the father." And he read firmly, "Rajahpur District, the Tennant family."

The Jays' elbows each found the other's ribs, giving a gentle poke. That meant the Robertses could take Celia home instead of sending her. This was fun, knowing the meanings of words that weren't there, the way Mugsy liked.

From the Book of the Jays December 17

One year ago we came here to stay a year. Now we are to stay longer. The bishop read it out yesterday. We all had surprises. The bishop had talked things over with Father before we went to see him! Father said he couldn't think of staying because he was sure the four of us would be happier at home. He hadn't asked us. The bishop said maybe fathers have things to learn, too.

But things won't be the same here, either, next year. Martha is taking Barby home, and they will travel with the Robertses. We don't have to move to that house. Barby is going to school in Berkeley and live with Aunt Gail. That cable came this morning. Martha will go to Jersey and see to our house—rent it, probably, so it will be lived in. Houses are better with people in them, Mother says.

And Jay and I are going to the hill school in March, with Mugsy. Father says we have been an example long enough, but our goats are a wonderful bunch of animals. Shaitan shines like silk. They are talking of giving Dhayan Singh the job of Superintendent of Animal Husbandry when he gets through at Government High School. We are teaching him out of the goat book now.

Martha is taking this diary to Miss Williams. So this is all we will write.

JT/1   JT/2